INFALLIBLE

VOL 1

TJ SPENCER JACQUES

NOVELS BY
TJ SPENCER JACQUES

NINE NOTCHES

BURGUNDY DOUBLOONS SERIES

INFALLIBLE SERIES

This is a work of fiction created by author TJ Spencer Jacques. All the characters, organizations, and events portrayed in this novel are either products of the author's imagination or used fictitiously.

INFALLIBLE

VOL 1

TJ SPENCER JACQUES

CHAPTER 1

Madden Night
Thursday, February 23, 2017
6:10 p.m.

Maybe I died and came back as a kite—or better yet, a satellite. I am drifting through the air on a floral printed comforter, sailing across New Orleans like "Meet George Jetson," like an emancipated genie who said *fuck the bottle*—waving at my haters like the King of Mardi Gras.

All my cares are miles behind, and I couldn't give a shit if a bubbling pond of lava was beneath me, because I'm high in the sky. I've never been this high before; this place where spooky gray curtains whisk across my face like sheets on a clothesline and cumulus swirls dance around my fingertips like dandelions in an April breeze. Is this my peak altitude? If it is, then let's "Sail On" like The Commodores to a land far away, where my worries are as thin as dove feathers and my joy is compressed like bales of cotton. Maybe I'll keep sailing due north until I reach heaven and show up unannounced like, *yeah, yeah, yeah*!

I'm not dressed for heaven.

I look like George Clinton's P-Funk.

Only the church folk would freak out—I think Jesus would dig it, though.

I wonder if he smokes?

You think he smokes?

Well, if there's no weed in heaven, then God can leave my black ass in New Orleans. *I'm straight.* Because I like people who like weed—that's why I'm high right now. *Oh shit, you felt that?* The room just dipped to the left. *Whoa, whoa, whoa!* I'm tripping, and I like it. I love it up here. I love this cloud. To form the perfect cloud, the conditions must be just right—meaning there has to be a perfect blend of three elements.

Fellowship.

A pound of fresh weed.

And the expert who rolls the perfect blunts.

I'm so blessed to have all three elements; a trifecta in perfect harmony with the cosmos, which means the blow is tight and the vibe is right. Tonight is Thursday night, that special evening each week we dedicate to *John Madden Football* on a PlayStation console and indulging in the best weed north of Columbia. I'm not sure how my little two-bedroom apartment on the Westbank of New Orleans became our tournament site every Thursday night, but it evolved that way over time.

It started out with just me and my wife's nephew, who we call Rasta Man for reasons you've probably figured out. We are the founding fathers of this *John Madden Football* tournament. My wife works from six p.m. to six a.m. at West Jeff Hospital—she's one of those labor and delivery nurses. On Thursdays, as soon as my wife is out the front door, but before she makes it to the first red light, Rasta lights the weed while I power up the PlayStation: then comes the cloud. A twelve-hour overnight shift is a lot of time for a man left to his own devices, and a sufficient amount of time to fumigate the living room.

Rasta's real name is Roderick Ross. When he converted to Rastafarianism three years ago, I was happier than a punk in a weave shop. Not because of the religion itself—to each their own—but any religion that promotes the smoking of weed is a good religion. Rasta's weed gives me life, but his wife Lauren grew up in a strict Pentecostal group called the Church of God in Christ, and she didn't appreciate the radical changes. She hated the dreadlocks, and she hated the little nuances like his nappy beard, his puffed tam caps, and his camouflage clothing for no apparent reason. When Rasta quit the FedEx job he'd held down for seven years, she divorced him before he made it home.

If you haven't guessed by now, Rasta is my connect for weed—that magical plant grown in God's backyard—and that's what friends are for: Dionne Warrick would agree.

What I love the most about Rasta is his weed is not for sale, which keeps me from having to go buy weed on the street and catching a charge from an NOPD in an unmarked car. And before I get too far ahead of myself, please allow me to clarify something: my nephew Rasta isn't a dope dealer, nor does he score dope. If Rasta has twenty pounds of weed, we smoke twenty pounds of weed.

"*I don't sell my medication,*" he always says.

All of this is fine with me, because Rasta has a home-grown grade of weed that's unlike anything I have ever smoked in my life—and I was a teenager in the seventies. Real talk though; the first time I took a hit off a blunt from Rasta, a naked munchkin appeared on my coffee table and started ass-clapping for fifteen minutes straight. No one else saw the munchkin but me. She had a chocolate complexion, dooky braids, and huge tits—true story.

All jokes aside, I love this brother—for real, not just for the unlimited supply of weed. Rasta is a good dude, and despite the failure of his marriage, he's a great father to his three boys. The other reason I love Rasta so much is because he's obsessed with *Madden Football*, as am I. Who could ask for anything more, right? Only problem with Rasta is if you beat him too many games in a row, he gets pissed off and packs up the weed.

There was a knock on my front door. After peeking out the front window, Rasta flicked our guest the bird. It was Telly. Rasta invited him into our group about two years ago, and it was Telly who started locking the door to keep Rasta's crybaby-ass from leaving. When I first met Telly, I was caught off guard because dude entered my apartment in a three-piece gray business suit with a purple bow tie.

I was like, "Rasta, you invited a pastor?"

Rasta was like, "Chill, he's not a pastor, this is my lawyer. Yah heard me?"

"He knows we smoke weed . . . right?"

(This conversation took place in front of Telly as if he were cellophane.)

"How do you think I pay my legal fees?" Rasta asked with a cheeky grin.

"In blunts?" I asked.

"In pounds!" Rasta nodded as he and Telly dapped.

Telly recently signed Rasta out of jail on a 9,500-dollar child support warrant that occurred because the court tried to serve him at his mother's address. His mom is notorious for refusing court papers and certified letters. She told the server, *Roderick don't live here and I ain't signing shit*. The arrears accumulated. In addition to the child support warrant, there was also the Possession with the Intent to Distribute charge Rasta caught three months prior.

At the end of every Madden Night, Telly collects his current legal fees from Rasta, minus the blunts he already smoked that evening. I always laugh my ass off as Rasta converts the poundage of the weed into currency, then deducts it from his overall bill. Nevertheless, that's Rasta, the most resourceful dude on planet Earth—and, as we've come to know him, the Wizard of Weed.

Rasta and Telly have the perfect partnership, because Rasta is always fighting a bullshit charge and Telly is always bailing him out and getting continuances on his upcoming court dates. Telly keeps Rasta out of jail, and Rasta keeps Telly high.

Perfect!

The two are old friends from high school, and they've been inseparable ever since. Despite being a lawyer, Telly checks his profession at the door when he enters my apartment and simply becomes one of the guys. Telly is tall as fuck—one of those guys who can bump his head on the ceiling fan light if he doesn't duck. He has one of those innocent faces, like that singer Brian McKnight, but Rasta told me that in court, Telly is mean as hell. He leads the local Bar in contempt of court arrests for challenging judges. But I understand Telly's foul disposition; if I went to school for all those years and my best paying customer was the weed man, I would be pretty pissed off, too.

The only time Telly smiles and lets loose is when he enters my house. That's when he transforms from an attorney into an annoying fucker we've branded as the Crowd Noise. Yes, that is his real nickname in our group: Crowd Noise.

How much shit do you have to talk to earn that name?

How annoying do you have to be to deserve such a name?

Just stick around and you will see for yourself—because it's tournament time.

While Rasta continued to roll a mound of quarter-sized blunts, it was time for me to fight my Green Bay Packers against Telly's Atlanta Falcons. As soon as the game started, I threw two interceptions; Telly returned both for touchdowns. I was behind 14–0 and there was no way to quiet his heckling ass.

"Didn't I tell you I was bringing these Falcons to burn down your fuckin' house? Didn't I tell you that? Huh! Huh!" he yelled in my ear. "This is my motherfuckin' house—yah heard me?"

I wanted to punch him in his face, but that too was part of his strategy—to aggravate you into making a mistake.

"Uncle Glenn, Uncle Glenn, Uncle Glenn! Your Packers ain't

shit. You selling ass cheap tonight . . . only two ninety-nine a pound." Telly raised my living room window. "Uncle Glenn selling ass cheap tonight! Flat ass, round ass, hairy ass, black ass, Latino ass . . . only two ninety-nine a pound!"

Selling ass was Telly's way of saying your team did not come to play. He was right, because I was higher than a light bill in July—beating Telly was the furthest thing from my mind. In the end, I lost that game 35–14, and was subjected to his bullshit for the rest of the tournament.

Over the years, I've grown to love Telly 'Crowd Noise' Ned, and I couldn't imagine Thursday nights without him.

Just as Rasta and Telly were about to kick off their game, a *bum-bum-bum-bum-bum* sound came from the front door. With controllers in hand, Rasta and Telly both shot me a look—*get the door.*

"Don't you Negros see me hopping out of this kitchen? You know who it is, go get the door."

Once on the patio, I forklifted the one-inch steaks out of the creole marinating sauce and gently laid each one on the grill. In my peripheral, I watched Rasta disappear down the hall again as he headed to the front door. I live in a two-story apartment complex off Woodland near what's known as the Cut-Off. The layout of my apartment is such that you enter through the front door, then continue left down a short hallway which opens to the living room.

The first piece of furniture that greets you in my living room is my 1994 gold-trimmed black lacquer entertainment center, with two china cabinet-like towers on each side of my fifty-six-inch flat-screen. My wife hates it, but I made up a lie and said that it was the only piece I had left from my grandmother. Inside one of the towers sits the CD player; we keep our wedding pictures in the other. Pressed against the wall across from the entertainment center is a deep blue, plush sofa, and cornering it to the right is the matching loveseat.

On the other side of the loveseat is the bar portion of the

counter, which gives entrance into the kitchen. Diana and I are the only two occupants of our two-bedroom apartment. I am the only person who sleeps in that second bedroom—on nights when I need a little privacy to watch porn.

Yes, I said porn.

Not to fantasize about the girls in the videos, but as a way to make sure I keep my fucking skills up to date. When you've been married for as long as I have, the only way to keep your dick updated without cheating is to watch porn. So, I watch sex tubes, then try new positions on Diana. Some of them she likes; the rest make her laugh.

"Glenn, you didn't hump like that when you were twenty-two, what are you trying to prove?" she asked yesterday morning.

"If you stop with the giggling . . . I'll show you," I fussed.

It was a position I saw in a video on Pornhub, where the guy positioned the girl on the corner of the bed, then pushed her forward facedown, ass-high.

It was then that he started turbo-humping her from the back. I even went through the hassle of counting the total number of rapid humps and the length of his intervals. After I watched the clip, I reviewed my notes and figured this must be the latest thing, so I popped a Blue Pill and set a goal to get in two hundred humps in two minutes, rest for thirty seconds, then follow it up with two hundred more. Diana was right—I damn near caught an asthma attack trying to update my dick, while she twisted in laughter.

Rasta returned to the living room with Jarvis, another member of our Madden Night brotherhood. Even though he is a teacher and subject to random drug tests, Jarvis smokes just as much weed as the rest of us. In *John Madden,* his favorite team is the Saints, and he would prefer taking a bath in a tub of piss over losing a game to Telly. When Telly and Jarvis face off, it marks the only time the room becomes silent. They're college buddies and compete to the death in just about everything in life, including *Madden*.

"Fuck those garbage-ass Saints," Telly called to Jarvis as he entered the room and embraced the crew.

"I will scar-drag you tonight until you change teams," Jarvis growled at Telly. "What's happening, Uncle Glenn? It's smelling good out there!"

"You know how I get down. I got the steaks laid, and the bills paid!" I yelled across the room. "Make sure you kick Telly's ass, he snuck me and fucked up my high. *Nigga did me dirty, dirty, dirty.*"

"Don't worry, Uncle Glenn, I came here with it on my mind tonight. Fuck Telly."

Jarvis removed his laptop his from tan leather bag and placed it in his normal place; on the kitchen table nearest to the outlet. Before Jarvis could power up, Telly destroyed Rasta by three touchdowns—it was going to be one of those nights. I entered the kitchen to find Rasta moving to the Loser Seat, which was actually the loveseat. Jarvis was up next.

"Jarvis, you don't want none. Don't you know Imma grown man, *bruh?* I'm a master of *Madden* . . . it's a video game but this shit ain't no game." Telly took a long drag off his blunt. "I'm hotter than charcoal tonight, nigga."

Crowd Noise was right, because Jarvis also lost by three touchdowns in the first half. That meant he was out for the night and had to cop a spot on the Loser Seat.

"HAVE A SEAT AND WATCH A GROWN MAN! IMMA NAPPY NUT MAN! YAH HEARD ME!" Telly let it be known.

And that right there was the reason you never wanted to drop a game to Telly 'Crowd Noise' Ned; the humiliation was unbearable. I almost forgot to mention that Jarvis is a writer. On most nights, he sits at the kitchen table with his laptop and stares at us like a crazy dude on the bus. I'm not sure what he's writing, but he says most of the time that he's grading papers—which is bullshit. If you ask me, I think he's documenting our personalities for a book, but he's *tight-lipped* about it. Jarvis is one of those writers who's always writing, but never has shit for you to read. If he is writing a book about us, then we're the best lab rats he's going to find—there's unlimited drama to write about. That's why he prefers to sit at my kitchen table, looking like a brokendown Will Smith.

He just returned to the kitchen to get his laptop, so I think it's time for me to threaten him again.

"You can write whatever you want, but if my name appears in that book and it messes up my Workers Comp, *I will kick your ass Jarvis!*"

"Unc, I'm not writing about you, because ain't shit about you interesting enough for a book," he laughed.

"All I know is I better not be in that book . . ."

Suddenly, our conversation was distracted for the fourth time that night.

Bum-bum-bum-bum-bum echoed from down the hall. Jarvis bolted across the room to answer the door as everyone took a blunt break from *Madden*. We all knew who it was; we were expecting him.

Front the kitchen, I heard Jarvis open the door—then it slammed shut.

"What the fuck?" Rasta yelled.

Then came the sound of a hard twist on the deadbolt lock. The person outside banged the door again like the DEA on a drug raid: *Bum-bum-bum-bum-bum*. Rasta snatched the blunts off the kitchen table and hauled ass to the bathroom.

Fearful it was the police, I yelled to Jarvis, "Who's at the door?"

Jarvis moseyed back to the kitchen table. "Some dude in a Direct TV shirt. I don't fuck with Direct TV. When it rains, the picture goes out!"

The room burst into laughter as I hopped down the hall to unlock the door. It was the fifth member of our Madden Night brotherhood—his name was Biyell.

"Quick! Somebody go knock on the bathroom door before Rasta scary-ass flushes all of that good weed down the toilet!" I panicked.

It was Jarvis who invited Biyell into the group two years ago, and he quickly became one of the brothers. Biyell is an installation contractor for Direct TV and Cox Cable, and always joins us at the end of his route. He could play *Madden Football* for fourteen hours a day if he didn't have to work. Biyell is another one of those dudes who hates to lose and always accuses one of us of using a cheat code on him. He's also one of those brothers who loves to fight over dumb shit, but so too are the rest of the guys, so he fits right in.

The guys love Biyell because he always has a funny story from his cable route. As soon as he starts the story of the week, Jarvis hauls ass to his laptop like a stenographer on a murder trial. Biyell never lets Jarvis down.

After greeting his way around the room and cursing out Jarvis for slamming the door in his face, Biyell reached for the controller.

"Why is it so quiet in here? Who died in this mutha-fucka? Where's Wayne?"

Biyell only listens to one rap artist, and if it isn't Lil Wayne, he doesn't want to hear it. Telly pressed play on Lil Wayne's *Tha Carter* album, and everybody yielded the floor to Biyell for the latest and greatest episode of the week.

"When she answered the door, Ms. Grandma had on a pink pantsuit like Hillary Clinton," Biyell explained as he lit his blunt. "I followed her through the house to the television she needed serviced, then I got down to business. About ten minutes later Ms. Grandma re-entered the room in a leopard-print robe that was loosely tied in the front."

"Get the fuck out of here, B!" Telly broke in.

"Serious shit," Biyell assured him before continuing. "In one hand she had this huge piece of chocolate cake, and in the other, a glass of white milk." Biyell scrolled through the list of teams until he found his Pittsburg Steelers.

"So, what happened after she slipped on something sexy for you?" Jarvis's nosey ass wanted to know.

"I said, *Ma'am, I have found your problem; looks like your dog may have chewed through your cable line, so I replaced it and plugged everything back in. It's working just fine now.* That's when Ms. Grandma—"

"What was her real name?" Jarvis interrupted.

"I believe it was Mary Brown or something like that; she was a white lady."

"*What fuckin'* difference does it make? We don't need to know her name," Telly complained. "Continue, *my-nigga,* continue."

". . . She walked over to me and said, *I have something else I need you to plug.*"

"No fuckin' way." Telly coughed up smoke.

"Then she asked me if I had a few minutes to spare. I was like, *why? For something sweet.* Then she handed me the big piece of chocolate cake and a chilled glass of milk. As I sipped the milk, she opened her robe full-view: matching leopard panties. I was like, damn . . . from the neck down she looked thirty years old. That cake was delicious."

"*But how was the pussy?*" I yelled from the kitchen.

Biyell appeared startled by my brashness. "Uncle Glenn!" Appalled, he leaped to his feet. "How could you ask me a bullshit question like that? Nigga, that woman was old enough to be my grandmother!" he frowned.

"*But how was the pussy?*" Rasta demanded to know.

After a short moment of reflection and six nods . . .

"The pussy wasn't bad . . . *not bad at all,*" Biyell confessed.

"NOOOOOO!" Telly yelled. "Tell me you didn't fuck that old lady."

"I was jumping in that pusssssssy like it was my birthday

party, and she was a bouncy castle." Biyell dry-humped the arm of my loveseat.

Rasta immediately fell to the floor and started rolling toward the entertainment center, while Jarvis laughed so hard he ran across the living room and continued out the front door.

"You potty dick fucka, you potty dick fucka!" Telly yelled as he wallowed on my sofa.

"I can't fuckin breathe," I heard Jarvis say. "Biyell, you fucked somebody's *grandmother!*" I was the only one left standing in the room.

We knew how the story would end, because at least once a week, Biyell fucked a customer on his route—sometimes two. I concluded it was his weekly goal to seduce at least one customer. Gasping for air, Jarvis re-entered the house, followed by the sixth and final member of our brotherhood.

"What da' fuck is so funny?" Timothy asked.

"It's another one of Biyell's *Potty Dick Cable Stories*," I replied.

"Don't tell me you took another pussy payment for free cable TV?" Timothy dapped off Biyell.

"*Is pig pork?*" I asked.

"*Did Ike Slap Tina?*" Rasta asked.

"Biyell, how much pussy is enough? For real bruh . . . ?" Timothy shook his head in pity as he walked over to embrace me. "Uncle Glenn, one day that nigga's dick is going to fall out his pants leg—dry rotted. Lady Diana is gonna be like, *what the fuck is this stuck in my brand-new vacuum cleaner? A dry rotten dick.*" Timothy pointed at Biyell. "With his nasty ass."

"Fuck you Timothy," Biyell paused his game. "I bet your fat ass hasn't seen your dick since 2008. Lose some weight and maybe a bitch would offer you some pussy once in a while.

"Fellas!" Biyell turned his attention back to the group, raised his glass, and requested his anthem. This meant we all had to stand for the anthem.

"Ain't not payment like a *pussssssy* payment, cause a *pussssssy* payment don't stop. Ain't no payment like a *pusssssy* payment cause a *pusssssy* payment don't stop!"

I hate that dumbass saying, but it's the cable man's anthem. If Biyell rolled up to your home to disconnect your cable for non-payment, a pussy payment got you a three-week extension—unless you fucked him again.

"*Ya heard me!*" Biyell swayed with a Cheshire-cat grin.

And it wasn't fair to the lonely little ladies on his cable route to have a guy like Biyell ring their doorbells, especially considering his God-given attributes. Dude was blessed with a natural S-curl, lightly toasted skin, a squared chin, deep blue eyes, a dimpled smile, and pecs that punched through his uniform shirt. And it wasn't just lonely old ladies who couldn't resist him—the majority of his conquests were married women. Like the episode last week—she was the pastor's wife, the wife of the same pastor who had baptized Rasta's sons.

According to Biyell, the married women on his route gave it up faster and more frequently than single women with less PFD: *Post-Fuck Drama.*

"And another thing, mutha-fucka," Biyell pointed his controller at Timothy. "What I do with my dick ain't your business— you better worry about this ass-whipping I'm going to put on those Patriots after I quiet this Crowd Noise." Biyell always had to have the last word.

Timothy was invited in over a year ago by Rasta. Timothy and Rasta grew up together, therefore he blended in perfectly with the rest of the crew. For Timothy, our Madden Night is more about smoking and conversation than it is about the game. Timothy's nickname is Cheating-Ass Cheater, because he plays as the New England Patriots. The computer always seems to hand him a victory somehow—it rarely fails.

During the day, Timothy is a freelance photographer in high

demand for weddings. Every week, he shares stories of photo-shoots with a supermodel-type cuties. The story is always the same: *The girl was so sexy, it was such a struggle to stay focused* . . . Tonight was no different.

"Guys, this girl today was stunning! She wasn't a model, but she came to me for professional photos. The longer the pho-toshoot went, the sexier she got. Nice, thick ass, with Tootsie Roll-colored skin, caramel eyes . . . Oh my God she was deli-cious." Timothy hit the blunt hard in her honor.

"*How was the pussy?*" Biyell wanted to know.

"Who me? Naw, pussy payments don't pay my studio bills."

"Shidddd! I couldn't have a job like that," Biyell admitted. "Sexy bitch come to me for a photo shoot—I'm snapping some dick in her! Turn to the right—snap, snap—*dick*! Turn to the left—snap, snap—*dick*!"

"We know, Biyell, we know!" I said above the locker room laughter.

"I'm serious, all of those *bad bitches* would get it . . ."

"We know, Biyell!" the group said.

Timothy is the CeeLo of the group, both in height and in that he's badly built, like an egg. What Timothy lacks in height he makes up for in Hollywood dreams. His goal is to develop a fea-ture film production company the likes of Lionsgate, and he of-ten breaks off into side conversations with Jarvis, since he loves to write.

Over the years, our Madden Nights became more than a weekly outing for a group of gamers; today, this place on Thurs-day nights is a bonding hub of brothers.

As you may have figured out, I'm the oldest of the bunch, which is why all of them call me Uncle Glenn. As I mentioned, Rasta is Diana's nephew. It's not often someone who just crossed fifty has the privilege to hang out with five younger brothers un-less he's coaching them in the NBA, but this has become my life squad. Before my horrific accident, I worked for Norfolk Southern Railway—before I needed to take a shit and had to use a porta potty on site. There I was, sitting on top of that poop bucket, praying none of that dark green water splashed on my ass . . . and that's when it happened.

Byron, my coworker—a twenty-something-year-old knucklehead who only got the job because his dad was three years past retirement, a guy whose pupils were as wide as nickels—backed a forklift into that porta potty, the one where I was taking that peaceful shit. The one where I was elevated high above that nasty green water.

That Byron.

That porta potty.

It tipped over with me inside. I nearly drowned in two weeks of piss and shit. But he didn't stop there—he rolled over my right foot, completely crushing it. When he finally heard my excruciating cry for help, I was a shitty mess to say the least. The doctors couldn't save my right foot, and if that weren't bad enough, I have to have monthly tests for the types of diseases common in people who have been exposed to sixty gallons of raw sewage.

And of course, it was later discovered that Byron had just taken a hit of heroin minutes before the accident. And of course, I sued for workplace injury, and for the fact that Byron wasn't required to take random drug test because of his father. The good news is, while I'm waiting for my lawsuit to drop, I get paid my full salary every week. Besides being an amputee, life is good.

Our weekly laughter was interrupted by the abrasive sound of rubber dragging across the pavement as something came to an abrupt halt. Then came the blaring of a horn that sounded more like a distressed lamb. Then the lamb was silenced by a loud thump. Seconds later, someone banged my door with the bottom of their fist.

I'd just handed Timothy a plate, so I was nearest to the door.

When I opened it, there was a tilted young woman in the doorway, standing with her arms tightly folded.

"Is Rasta here? I know he is . . ."

"Well hello to you, too." I couldn't remember her name, but she remembered mine.

"Sorry Uncle Glenn . . . how are you? You have to excuse me . . . it's just, I'm so pissed right now. Please call Rasta for me."

"I'll get him for you, and your name is?"

"He knows who in the fuck this is!" she yelled at me, and that's when I remembered her.

It was Shameka!

CHAPTER 2

Madden Night
8:30 p.m.

Her words were preheated, like the steam above a pumpkin spice latte. Her crayon-brown skin was tight, and her feline, hazel eyes gleamed in the wintery night. That little ravine between her pencil-tip eyebrows guided me to a waterfall of licorice hair, which cascaded down the center of her back—damn near to her ass from what I could tell. Shameka was thick and sexy. Her praline leather pants made her legs appear moist. My mouth watered like I was a kid in a candy store. She was gorgeous. She was delicious. And believe me, I tried to look away—every muscle in my neck strained to turn my head—but I made the mistake of looking down instead.

That embossed triangle.

That purring fat cat.

That camel toe.

It was the girl from the porn video last night. I'm tripping, it wasn't, but Shameka was just as fine. *Stop looking at her pussy print,* I heard a voice say. *You're married.*

But it was just a peek; it's not like I touched her or anything like that. After all, that's Rasta's girl.

That's how it starts, the voice said. *Stop peeking.*

All right. All right. Even from a distance, when you're married, you can't appreciate a fine woman.

But you already have a fine woman.

OKAY, geez! I said to the voice in my head. Then I hopped down the hall to call Rasta. I entered the living room to find Jarvis's nosey ass *looka-whoing* out the window with Timothy next to him.

"Rasta, Jennifer Hudson is at the door," I announced.

"Who?" Telly asked.

"It's Shameka," I said. "And she's here to kick your ass."

"I'm not for this tonight . . ." Rasta huffed as he moseyed to the door.

"Should we pause the game and pray for you?" Telly joked.

Rasta ignored him with a flimsy wave. "She aggravates me to no end!"

"Don't be out there with all that bullshit in front of my door," I said. "We're good Christian folk around here." Rasta dismissed me with another flimsy wave.

No sooner did Rasta greet her at the door than Shameka lit into him.

"Who in the fuck is LaDeisha?" her voice boomed through the hall.

"Who?" he played dumb.

"LaDeisha. Who in the fuck is she?"

"Shameka—Shameka, let's have a seat in my truck . . . and talk this over."

"Talk, my ass!"

"Chill, please," Rasta tried to calm her. "Lower your voice before you cause a scene in front of the neighbors."

"Fuck these neighbors: *who is LaDeisha?*" Shameka stabbed Rasta in the chest with a stiff finger.

Down the hall to my left, Jarvis hopscotched in front of the window as the mess and drama unfolded while Timothy reached for his cell phone. "If she starts kicking his ass . . . I'm recording all of it."

Rasta reached for her arm and tried to escort her to his truck. Shameka snatched her arm from his grip.

"A woman was in my shop today, and your name came up. Apparently, you're dating her daughter."

"Dating her daughter?"

"You heard me—her daughter."

"No way was she referring to me, this has to be a misunderstanding."

It wasn't a misunderstanding. Rasta knew it, and now Shameka knew it. She'd just discovered that Rasta had another woman, and that she was what I call an accidental mistress; an unbeknownst sister wife, or in some parts of the hood, a deceived side chick. The only problem was that Rasta hadn't informed her that she was the mistress. His 'main' girl is LaDeisha; they're not married because he has this little issue with child support. LaDeisha doesn't want to be on the hook for his payments, and Rasta's ex-wife is the kind of woman who would serve her with a court summons if she could: to collect twenty-eight extra dollars a month.

There's also the issue of LaDeisha's mother, who is serving her fifth term in Congress. Her mother took one look at Rasta and was instantly opposed to him. LaDeisha is being prepped for a House Seat in the Louisiana legislature, and the last thing her mother wants is for Rasta's lifestyle to fall in the hands of a political opponent.

Back to Shameka.

She runs a nail shop out of her house on Gov. Nichols, and she co-signed for Rasta's truck—the same truck he uses to haul his African-themed wood products to the flea markets every day. When Rasta shared his dream of owning his own woodworking warehouse where he could also mass-produce his cabinets and countertops, Shameka conducted the research and typed up his business plan. She was all in for him, and now she's all out here, ready to kick his ass.

Biyell and Telly paused their game to listen to the argument, while Jarvis and Timothy bent my venetian blinds. I watched as Biyell walked over to the window and squeezed in to the left of Jarvis. Telly hovered and demanded the play-by-play. As for me, it wasn't that I didn't want to partake in the drama, but I had steaks on the grill out back which were far more important than Rasta and Shameka. I hopped my crippled ass to the back of the house as quickly as I could and re-basted my steaks, then hurried back to the front to see if Rasta had managed to get Shameka to calm down.

Not even close.

"You don't have to take that shit, Rasta!" Timothy yelled through the closed window.

"Don't let her handle you like that, Rasta man!" Crowd Noise bucked him up.

"See, that's why I only fuck with BBWs; I don't have these problems." Biyell offered.

"Oh, oh! She popped the trunk! Oh, oh! There go his clothes all over the street, oh my!" Jarvis laughed.

I hopped to the front door, because all four guys were jousting for position in the window. That's when I saw Rasta collecting his clothes off the pavement. Several neighbors who I've only interacted with in passing seemed thrilled by the spectacle; some reclined on their balconies. When she wasn't tossing his clothes everywhere, Shameka punched and slapped Rasta—but he's a lover, not a fighter.

I cracked the door just a little more to hear the argument.

"Shameka, why are you acting like this? Look at all the people watching you make a scene," he tried to reason with her.

"Fuck those people! You weren't worried about what *people* might think when you started fucking with *LaDayyyysha*. Did you give a fuck then?" Her entire body rolled with her neck. "Huh? Did you give a fuck?"

"Meka, how do you fly off the handle like this? At least ask me about it first—"

"It was you, and you know it. She called you by name. She knew the color of your truck, and that you work in the French Market. Motherfucker, it was you." A swing, a duck, and a miss. Then a kick that landed on both nuts. Down went Rasta. She stood over him like Ali.

"The worst part was, I had to bite my tongue while they talked because I had a customer in the chair, but I'm not stupid—she was talking about you."

"Shameka, I don't know a LaDeisha . . ." he groaned slowly to his feet.

"I must look like a stupide *hoe* to you? Is that it?"

"No, I'm not calling you stupid; I don't know LaDeisha."

"Bullshit."

Shameka opened the rear passenger door and threw another bundle of his clothes across the parking lot.

"Those messy bitches in my nail shop confirmed that you were fucking with a bitch named LaDeisha. If that's where you want to be, if that's who you want to be with, then go be great, nigga! But not in my truck and not in my house." Shameka threw the last of his things on the pavement. All of Rasta belongings were just about everywhere.

"Meka, just hear me out . . ."

"Fuck that . . . hand me the keys to my F150!"

It was time for me to intervene, so I asked Jarvis to fix Shameka a steak plate and wrap it. I had to ask him twice, because he couldn't pull himself away from the window. With the plate in hand, I hopped out to her.

"How are you, Shameka?"

"Oh, you remember me now?"

"Yes, but your hair was short when I first met you, and you know I'm getting old."

"Uh-hm, forgetting a bitch must be an airborne disease around here."

"Shameka, I don't know a LaDeisha . . ." Rasta pleaded.

"Uh-hm. So I am a stupid hoe to you? Huh?!" She placed her cell phone on the hood of her car.

"Shameka, Shameka!" I jumped back in. She started to remove her earrings, it was escalating. "I have some extra steak, here is one off the grill with some potato salad. I also have sweet tea, Hennessy, Crown, and—"

"I'm good. Now if you would excuse us, this cheating nigga was just about to hand me my keys."

For the second time, I offered her the plate. *Success.* The aroma from the sizzling-hot steak seeped through the foil and traveled up to her nose. It weakened her. I witnessed the moment her breathing slowed and her eyes made contact with the hot plate. She wanted that steak.

"I'll take the Hennessy," she said.

When I returned with the cup of Hennessy, Shameka gave me a sideways hug, then whipped her hair at Rasta. Seconds later, she burned rubber out of the parking lot. Rasta was able to keep his truck for now, but his night of bullshit was long from over. It was time to face the fellas.

Under the gossiping eyes of my neighbors I helped Rasta collect his things off the ground. Once inside the house, all five of the guys were standing in a single-file line holding Walmart bags stretched open.

"Here's some Gucci luggage for all your stuff." Biyell offered a bag.

"Man, fuck y'all," Rasta mumbled his way back to the living room.

"Wyclef Jean, how you let Jennifer Hudson kick your ass like that?" Timothy asked.

"She was just showing off . . . that's all. Watch when I get over to her place later, it will be a different story."

"Her place?" Jarvis asked. "Dude, I would steer clear of her for a while, unless you want more of your shit tossed outside."

The roast was on.

"Serious shit, Rasta, if you need to catch a sofa for a few days so she can't find you, I got you," Timothy offered.

"Tim, you think you're slick?" Telly honed in. "You trying to gain exclusive rights to the weed."

Pretty much every mistress has a code name; the way she's identified within the crew. Shameka is usually just referred to as Shameka, although she can be recognized as Jennifer Hudson as well. Everyone here has a mistress except me. I only have my wife, Diana. The guys call her Lady Diana, and she is more than enough. Next month will make twenty-five years we've been together; twenty-four of the happiest years of my life. In Diana, I truly have everything a man could want and need. She only has two more years on that job before retirement, and our plan is to take a long train ride across country and have sex all day in a rail car—I can't wait. I know I'm much older than these guys, and I'm not perfect, but I wish they would give this one-woman thing a try; it's less headache, and in Rasta's case, less humiliation.

It was Rasta's turn against Timothy, and in the first quarter his Buffalo Bills were already down 14–0. If Tim and those cheating Patriots score again, the game is over. Wouldn't you know it—a pick six touchdown for the Patriots! Game over!

"Man, I'm not in it tonight . . ." Rasta admitted.

"Dude, if my drawls were all over the parking lot, I wouldn't be into it, either. I'm not trying to tell you how to handle your shit, but she took that too far," Jarvis suggested.

"Yeah, you right. I'm about to go check her for handling me like that and showing her ass!"

"Dude, chill right here and let things cool off or Telly will be bailing your ass out of jail on another charge." I handed Rasta a beer. "You can't pour cold water in a hot radiator; let the damn thing cool off . . . then crank it," I suggested. "Take Tim up on his offer if you think she's going to come around your place, and leave the weed with me," I laughed.

Around ten o'clock, it was time to shut it down. I watched as all of them checked in with the other women in their lives, getting in the last of their sweet nothings for the evening. The mistresses received the flirtatious phone calls while their wives received a dry text saying, *I'm on my way home*. That's when I hit them all with a little something to think about.

"Look at you bunch of man-whores. What if you walked in your bedroom tonight and found a dude pulling twelve inches of dick out of your woman—how would you handle it?"

"You nut in it, you own it," Jarvis said.

"I would stand right there in the doorway and wait until they finish. When he leaves, he better take that bitch with him," Telly said.

"Both of them motherfuckers dying right there!" Biyell said. "Shot dead in mid-hump."

"Dude, you would really spend the rest of your life in prison over pussy?" Telly asked.

"Fuckin' right, mutha-fucka, come in my house trying to steal some pussy—I have to kill him for disrespecting me. Then fucking her . . . in my bed? I wish a motherfucker would."

"I ain't saying I would kill 'em, but you could bet on close to death. That's some foul shit on her part, but these women are niggas too," Timothy said.

"What about you, Rasta—if you walk up on some bullshit in your bed how would you handle it?"

Rasta took a long hit off his blunt and passed it to Telly. "Shameka's pissed off right now but she wouldn't go there on me. She's not that type."

"That's what you think, Rasta; all of them are that type," Biyell powered down the PlayStation. "Do you have any idea how many married women I fuck on random? Their husband's thinking it's his pussy while I'm punishing her with this elephant trunk. Trust me when I say it, if the conditions are right, all of them are that type."

"Rasta, all I'm saying is, have a game plan for everything—even a plan to remain calm should you walk in on something tonight, tomorrow, or next month. In my experience, when a woman is that pissed off, some of them give away what I call *mad pussy*. That's what happened to me; my ex-girlfriend said she was trying to make me feel what she felt when I got busted. I told her, *You can't get me back by fucking some dude!*" Telly had actually caught his ex in his bed fucking her boss. "Rasta, just give me your word—you will stay calm not matter what," Telly pleaded.

They shook hands.

From my kitchen table, Jarvis's messy ass was typing so fast his laptop sounded like microwave popcorn. This was the type of story and drama he loves; how that dude hasn't written a best-seller with just the madness that takes place amongst us is puzzling. Every week it's something new. This week it just happens to be Rasta, but I promise if you stick around, you will see why we say *it goes down on Madden Night*. See you next Thursday.

CHAPTER 3

Madden Thursday
March 2, 2017
4:10 p.m.

She pranced around the house in panties and a tank top while waiting for the dryer to iron out all the wrinkles, I guess you have to be a *man-ish* man to appreciate this view. After she heard the dryer timer, she hurried to the wash room and then returned to the foot of the bed. That's when the show began. One of the privileges of being a man is watching your woman's booty disappear into a pair of pants. It's my favorite part—the scrubs. Yes, I said scrubs, as in those turquoise, string-fastened outfits, the kind worn by hospital staff. I freaking love them, and her scrubs are just below the booty. She dipped her hip left, then right, and just like that, the booty was gone until morning.

"Mmmmm, mmmmm, mmm! Let me squeeze it one more time before you go!" I begged.

My wife Diana isn't thick, she isn't skinny; she's *slim fine*.

"There you go, every time I'm getting ready for work you it's *mmmmmm,* because you know I don't have time."

"I'm just checking you out. Liking what I see. Patting myself on the back. Just trying to holler at you . . . that's all."

"Hmm, I hear you, Glenn." She applied lotion to her neck and arms. "I'm beginning to think you're scared of me. The *nasty talk* doesn't start until I'm about to leave." She tried on earrings in the large mirror above the dresser.

"Who me?" I pointed at my chest. "Scared of you?"

"Yes, scared of little ole me," she puckered.

"Diana, please! Keep talking shit, you're going to wake up *Big Bad Buck.* Remember last time, when he threw you on the floor and took some? Keep talking shit."

She loved when I attacked her as Big Bad Buck, my slave alter ego. I'd barge in on her and say something crazy like, *massa told me to snatch youz up and make some childruns.* Diana would then run around the apartment while I hopped behind her. Then she'd fall down with her legs wide open like a white woman in a scary movie.

"Come on, try it, I dare you!" Diana pulled the string on her scrubs, then bent over the dresser and wiggled. "Here you go, Big Bad Buck, I'm right here, come take me!"

The truth was, my dick hadn't recovered from this morning, it was only at thirty percent charged. "You're lucky you have to go to work, I would—"

"I can call in. Come on Big Bad Buck, I thought massa sent you to take my goodies!" Diana pulled up her scrubs and tied the strings. "*You all talk and no dick.*" She finished applying her mascara.

After I recovered from laughing, I hopped behind her as she prepped in the mirror. Her neck reclined on my chest. My arms wrapped around her waist. There we stood fused in the mirror, admiring each other like we were on our first date. I have been blessed with good women, but it was always the right them, wrong me. I know this sounds crazy to you, but there are a few women in my past who truly deserved this Glenn—the one that's satisfied and focused. And I know you're thinking it's wrong to have thoughts about other women while holding my wife, but it's appropriate. Without those failures, I would have never landed safely here, with Diana.

Like other couples, we have our share of good days and bad days. What sets us apart is we've reached a plateau where we no longer care who wins the argument, as long as there's a compromise and the peace is respected. Not many women who dreamed of owning their own home would've settled for renting an apartment, but Diana did it for me. Not many women could handle a man going from a picture of perfect health to an amputee, but she suffered it for me and cared for me. Not many women would have stayed with a man after public scandal and shame—having her entire family shun her for loving me—but she endured it for me.

Teddy Pendergrass once said, *It's so good loving somebody when somebody loves you back*, and that's what we have. Like Angela Bassett, Diana can play whatever role I need, from Tina Turner to Coretta Scott King; she takes the stage for her man. Just below my chin, I heard a deep sigh

"After all of these years, you still have that look . . . for me."

"Years? It's been years?"

She blushed. "How time flies when you're having fun?"

"Yes it does. Speaking of having fun, in the morning we need to have a little talk."

"About?"

"This new thing you're into."

"What new thing?" She started to blush again.

"You know, that hair thing, and the threats . . ."

Her Hershey-colored skin turned candy-apple red. "What hair thing?"

"You need a reminder? *Pull it Pull it!*"

"Sorry, you must have me confused with someone else." Like a bashful doe, she darted into the bathroom and tried to shut me out, but I was in high pursuit. I teased her through the door frame.

"So you don't remember yelling, *either fuck me like you missed me or get out?*"

Diana managed to slam the door. On the other side, I heard the squeaking of her curling iron barrel, followed by the swoosh from a spray bottle.

"So I guess you don't remember? Maybe it was a wild woman from my dream."

"Or one of your porn bitches." I heard a girlish chuckle.

"No, it was you, sneaking the freak out instead of giving it to me all at once."

"You should thank me."

"Oh really, and why should I thank you?"

"Because I'm trying not to kill you . . . with this *pusssssy.*" There was an evil hiss in her voice.

"Kill me with it, I dare you!" We continued to laugh on opposites sides of the door.

After about five minutes, the knob twisted, and I lost my breath again. Her lips gleamed with a light gloss, her eyes were refreshed, and the room was filled with a royal fragrance, like little flower girls had dropped pedals around my bed. Her scent was rich, like in the interior of a brand-new Bentley; something sweet and a dab of something new. Not that I've driven one, but she smelled how I imagine a new Bentley would smell.

With my arm against the door frame, I blocked her escape. "Care to explain?"

"Glenn, Glenn, Glenn, my sweet adorable husband, when it comes to freakiness just remember one thing. You look at porn to get ideas, and I let you have that little vice, but if you had the chance to see my thoughts, you would never watch another video," Diana said in her Southern Belle voice. Then, she gave me a micro-kiss on the lips and ducked under my armpit.

Before I could turn completely around to hop after her, she grabbed her purse and ran to the front door. I hopped behind her as fast as I could, but not fast enough. At the door, she pulled the drawstring on her scrubs once more and wiggled her pink cotton work panties. I was like a one-legged frog trying to get to her, but she knew the safe distance to taunt me.

Just as I made it to her, she pulled up the scrubs, tied the string, and bolted out the door. Through the window, I waved. Through the windshield, she flicked an X-rated tongue, then shifted her car into reverse. By the time I made it back to the living room, I heard my cell phone chirp; it was a text from my wife.

Enjoy your Madden Night tonight.

Enjoy your shift tonight, I texted back.

The next time I tell you to fuck me hard and pull my hair you better do as I say! Are we clear, Big Bad Buck?

I couldn't stop smiling.

Yes, we're clear.

I'm not sure if it's a phase, but whatever has gotten into my wife, I like it and I want more of it in the morning. My dick should be at ninety-nine percent by then.

CHAPTER 4

Madden Night
6:30 p.m.

Tonight for Madden Night, the menu is barbecue leg quarters, baked macaroni, stuffed bell peppers, and a pan of banana pudding. Not that fake banana pudding they make on the food network with Jell-O pudding and wafers, but the old school where you cook the cream, add vanilla extract, and enough sugar to give you diabetes with the first spoonful. That's how we eat in New Orleans: *Chew now and worry later.*

And if you're wondering why my wife is so understanding about Madden Night, then I just gave you a hint: the food. Every week the guys toss up ten to twenty dollars each for the food and drinks for next week, and my job as host is to cook everything and chill it in time for the tournament. Every week after Madden Night, she has leftovers for her lunch for the next three days, and that's why she tolerates it. Being that I love to cook and they love to eat, it's a win-win. Every week, it's the same routine all the way down to the music, only Lil Wayne, only Jay-Z, sometimes Juvenile, once in a while Master P, then right back to Lil

Wayne and Jay-Z! The first *Carter* album by Lil Wayne and the *Black Album* by Jay-Z. Only!

If you want to see a fight, then play something other than the aforementioned. All hell will break loose and someone will peg the change-up in song as the reason they lost the game. For real, they are just that anal retentive about those two albums—from 2004.

The first to arrive was Jarvis.

Our stenographer immediately plugged in his laptop. He looked a little wide-eyed. Something was bothering him, but whatever it was, it didn't look all bad. His face went from cloudy to sunshine every two minutes. If the truth be told, I am just as nosey as Jarvis, but I don't write everything down—I save it in my mental file until I need to make a point or back somebody the fuck up . . . but I digress.

"What's going on with you today? One of those students kicked your ass again?"

A few months ago, Jarvis showed up for Madden Night with a black eye as a result of trying to break up a fight between two students. He'd jumped in the middle of the wind-milling girls and caught a right hook in his face. Dude's eye was so black he looked like a pirate.

"Jarvis, it looks like you finished fucking a ghost? What's up?"

Jarvis shook his head. "Man, man, man!"

"Man, man what?"

"Man!"

"Bro, what's going on with you?" I yelled from the kitchen.

"I don't even know where to start."

"Start somewhere, just give me a second to catch a seat."

Before he could get a word out, I reminded myself that I was dealing with a thirty-eight-year-old male who resembles Will Smith, got married too young, and worked at a high school full of horny teachers. The difference between Biyell and Jarvis is Biyell will admit he's dicking down his customers; Jarvis, on the other hand, is sneaky with his creep life. Whatever this was, I knew it had to be something related to knocking up one of those young teachers at that high school.

"Last week I told you I went to the Krewe of Zulu Carnival Ball . . . right?"

"Yeah, I remember—that ball where y'all pay and bring your own food and hide it under the table . . . that ghetto-ass ball."

"It's not ghetto, it's tradition."

"Ghetto tradition . . . but I remember." The oven timer sounded on my bell peppers.

"Well, my wife has a table she sponsors at the ball for her family and friends. We do this every year but, but, but . . ."

"But what?" I yelled from the kitchen as I removed the pan of stuffed bell peppers out of the oven.

He started shaking his head again. "But this year my wife had to leave early—she wasn't feeling well. I wanted to leave with her, but she asked me to stay in her place and continue to host refreshments."

"I never understood that bring-your-own-food bullshit, but to each its own."

"Glenn, stay with me. I walked my wife to the car, and when I made it back to the ball, everyone was on the dance floor. And then the lights went dim. The guest performer was Fantasia. Standing in front of me watching Fantasia was Briana—"

"Bri who?"

"My wife has this niece—she's twenty-six years old, fine as fuck, pretty as fuck . . ."

"And young as fuck! And family as fuck!" I checked Jarvis.

"I know, I know, that's why I was so caught off guard when she started grinding her ass on me. At first I thought she could've confused me with someone else, but then she reached for my hands and wrapped them around her waist. It was like a lap dance standing up."

"No one saw you two dry humpin'?"

"No, because the crowd was packed in tight around the stage, and we were in the darkest area by the wall. Uncle Glenn, she seduced me and I liked it. She was so hot! For three consecutive love songs, she rubbed her cotton-soft ass on me until my dick touched my shoes."

"Jarvis, you can't read too much into that because that's how these young girls dance these days; they let you feel it all . . . right on the dance floor."

"I concluded the same thing, but after the song was over, she thanked me for the dance and whispered in my ear, *I've wanted you for a long time.* You could have laid me on the ground and pissed on me—I wouldn't have blinked. I was just that blown away."

"The niece we're talking about, she's on your wife's side of the family?"

"Yes, my sister-in-law Connie has three daughters, and this is the youngest one. But it gets better. Once the ball was over and everything was packed in my truck, guess who pulled on side my car?"

"Briana . . ."

"She did this little thing with her finger and the next thing you know, I followed her!"

"To where?"

"Her apartment!"

"*How was the pussy?*" Biyell asked as he picked up a PlayStation controller.

"Huh?" Jarvis seemed caught off guard.

I saw Biyell when he walked in, but Jarvis didn't, and there was no need to interrupt this juicy bit of mess to speak to Biyell's bunk ass.

"What pussy?" Jarvis replied to Biyell.

"You heard me! *How. Was. The. Pusssssay?*"

Jarvis's body shook from a suppressed laugh he couldn't hold. "Bruh . . . the pussy was fire!"

"I knew it, I knew you fucked her! I said it to myself when you told the part about the slow dance, and all that romantic shit.

I was like *nigga get to the part about the pussy!*" Biyell laughed.

"That young girl fucked me, bruh, for real. I've had my share of women just like you guys, but there is something about when a woman desperately wants you inside of her—nothing compares. I didn't make it home until three in the morning. Monica was asleep, but I couldn't sleep. All I thought about until the dawn was how good she fucked me—until I was empty."

"Who fucked you?" Timothy asked.

"What's up Tim?" I yelled.

"What's happening, Uncle Glenn! Jarvis, who fucked you?" Tim wanted to know.

"Dude done *bust off* in a young one!" Biyell answered.

"A young one?" Crowd Noise Telly arrived. "Oh shit . . . who done pulled an R. Kelly?"

"Feeling on her bo-bo-booooty!" I sang.

"I knew it was coming. I just said the other day—one of these days imma turn on the news and see your ass handcuffed for fucking one of those students," Biyell said.

"I didn't fuck a student!" Jarvis yelled. "It was my niece and she's twenty-six!"

"That's even worse! Why fuck your niece and not one of those fine-ass teachers I saw at your Christmas party?" Telly asked.

"Nigga, she's not my blood related niece!" Jarvis replied in disgust.

"He fucked his wife's twenty-six-year-old niece!" Biyell yelled out.

"Wait! Wait! You fucked Monica's niece?" Rasta dropped 224 grams of weed on the coffee table. "Since when we fuck nieces? We don't fuck nieces! Dude, why are you fucking your niece? All the grown pussy out here . . . you fucking your niece . . ." Rasta was getting angry.

"FOR THE HUNDREDTH TIME, she's not my niece for real, but by marriage, and she's almost thirty years old," Jarvis explained.

"Over stand, over stand," Rasta nodded.

"You fucked your niece? You dirty dick fucka!" Crowd Noise yelled. "Let me see a picture of her!"

That was about all the condemnation Jarvis received. After he showed them her picture, most of them understood how he got caught up, and the others were more concerned with the mountain of weed on my coffee table. I sat and listened to Jarvis tell the same story from the top, to clear up that he didn't set out to fuck his niece, but she offered him. I'm not saying that Jarvis was right for fucking his niece, but I do believe his account of the story. I could tell from his face that he didn't set out to do it, and if this was something he'd planned, then we would have known about that plan.

Even as he told the story, you could still tell that Jarvis was living a fantasy. Maybe not with this girl, but with who-knows-how-many women at work he wanted to fuck, only to have a twenty-six-year-old with a flaming *hot cat* rock his world. My challenge is, how do I get Jarvis to come down off this high before he destroys his entire life as he knows it?

"And right as I was getting ready to nut she got down and—"

I interrupted. "Jarvis, let me ask you a question."

"UNCLE GLENN, WHAT THE FUCK?! HE WAS GETTING TO THE GOOD PART!" Crowd Noise Telly lost it.

"Uncle Glenn, for real dude! It can wait!" Biyell snapped at me.

"Your timing is always fucked up, Unc!" Timothy laughed.

"She got down and . . . what?" Biyell paused the game and waited for Jarvis to continue the story.

"Jarvis, if your wife catches you with this girl, is this someone you can be with for the rest of your life?" I asked. A hush suffocated the room.

I was on the verge of blowing their high, but I had to ask him. I had to gain a better understanding of where this was going. The reason I grew so concerned was because Jarvis had the look—it was a star-struck gaze as if he'd just received an autograph from the greatest pussy the world has ever known. Mentally, he was gone for the summer, and I knew my window to talk some sense into him was quickly closing.

At some point during the entire experience with Briana, Jarvis felt it—whether a familiar intimacy or sex from a distant galaxy, that young woman took him there and left him. Jarvis did not want to come back to Earth, back to his wife, back to his reality . . . and I saw it in his eyes. So, while the guys were entertained by this story, a bright red *Check Engine* light glowed in the center of his forehead as he continued on a joyride to Divorceville.

The good news was the cloud that hovered from the five blunts in my living room—blunts that puffed like steam irons in a dry cleaner's. Both PlayStation controllers rested in the middle of the coffee table, looking abandoned, feeling forgotten. The star of the evening was Jarvis. All heads faced Jarvis, and every dick in the room (except mine) dreamed of being his dick, diving in and out of this sexy young woman; vicariously in taboo-ish bullshit, though none of them would confess.

I gave my oven a break for the night and placed a tray of crab cakes on the counter. Jarvis was on a hook and I was reeling him back when Timothy gave him a way of escape.

"Y'all hear that?" Timothy asked. "That's the sound of my dick committing suicide! How do you mention the word *wife* in the middle of a story like that? Huh! Huh! I'm almost forty but I look fifty—I can't pull a twenty-year-old hot piece of ass anymore. Jarvis, please carry on and fuck Uncle Glenn's question." Timothy was perturbed.

"Jarvis, I'm serious, I know you said she's fine . . ."

"Correction, he said fine as fuck!" Timothy corrected me.

"And I know you said she's pretty . . ."

"Correction, he said the bitch is Beyoncé-level!" Biyell corrected me.

". . . But if your wife catches you with her, can you do life with Briana?"

Every head in the room turned in the opposite direction. It was like I had the worst breath in New Orleans. If they could have kicked me out of my own house, at that moment my ass would have been tossed on the pavement like Rasta's drawls. They didn't want to consider it; that question was like rat poison to Chucky Cheese, but the question was a valid one.

"Okay, I will give you a moment to think on that one, while I reload another. Since the Zulu ball last week, how many times have you slept with Briana?" Wouldn't you know it, heads started to turn back in my direction.

"Six . . ."

"DAMN!!!!" I was astonished. "SIX!"

"Now that's what I'm talking about—yum-yum that pussy!" Biyell fist-bumped. "Jarvis, everyday?" Telly asked. "You can still fuck every day?"

"Hmmm, sure. Can't you?" Jarvis asked.

"I haven't fucked every day since I was nineteen!" Telly replied.

"That's because your dick prefers weed over pussy." I said. The room laughed.

"Tru dat . . . tru dat!" Telly agreed as he took another long drag off his blunt. "But you actually want pussy every day?"

"Not normally, just with Briana. It amazed me, too. I busted one, then was hard again. That shit never happened with my wife, even before she took sick, but this girl has me so excited. And I never received so many wet pussy pictures in my life. All day at work, she sends me videos of her wet fingers sliding in and out—"

"Let me see," Biyell requested.

"Hell no!" Jarvis replied. "I show you this video I would have to shoot you."

I interrupted Biyell's pleas to see the videos. "If Monica catches you with Bri-Bri, could you do life with her?"

And that's how the mistresses received their code names. From that night forward, she was *Bri-Bri*, Rasta's girl was *Steak*, and Timothy's girl was *Tootsie*. You will meet the other mistresses a little down the line, but back to Jarvis.

"To be honest, Uncle Glennn, the pussy feels good enough to do life with her, but all hell would break out if my wife ever caught me with this girl. Y'all would be dancing with my coffin on your shoulders like that YouTube video."

That's all I wanted Jarvis to do—at least think about life after getting caught with Bri-Bri. Not only was it infidelity, but the impact to Monica's side of the family was not worth the risk. But I just allowed you a sneak peek into how shit started that should never have started. With the exception of Rasta Man, pussy is the guys' drug of choice. Some of them manage their addictions, while others are managed by their addictions. Don't get me wrong—I love sex just as much as they do, but I love the one who wiggled her cute booty at me this morning, and Diana is my drug.

I often wonder why one woman isn't enough for them. It's not like Jarvis has an ugly wife—I think she is drop dead gorgeous even with her health issues. But they've been together since high school, so one could use the fickle excuse that sometimes the things a man likes at nineteen are no longer the things they like at thirty-eight.

This is why I advise women never marry a man in his twenties—his brain is still developing and he doesn't know what he wants or who the fuck he is! If you marry a man from ages twenty to thirty-eight, be prepared to walk through seventy-eight miles of dog shit in a brand new pair of Christian Louboutin's red bottoms.

"So it's over? You've gotten it out of your system, fulfilled the fantasy of dicking down a young one, and now you're ready to move forward . . . right?" I had to ask, but I knew the answer.

"After tonight, I will let her go."

"I hear you." He's hooked.

"And what's it to you if that man wants to put his *wee-wee* in the *Bri-Bri?* She gave it to him!" Biyell's ignorant ass yelled at me.

"Wait, hold up, so after tonight that makes seven times you fucked her?" Telly was still stuck on Jarvis fucking her every day. "I mean, your shit didn't go down? Not one time? It stayed hard all six days?"

"Telly! Is there something you want to share with the group, because sounds like you're having pipe problems!" Timothy laughed.

"No, I'm not saying that. My dick works just fine, I'm just asking."

"Your shit not getting hard, huh Telly? You can't put it in sometimes, huh Telly? That pussy be laughing at you, huh Telly?" Timothy taunted.

They all went in on Telly.

"Your dick softer than a belt on a bath robe, huh Telly?" Biyell asked.

"Telly smoke so much weed I bet when he nut, smoke comes out first!" Rasta joined in the roast.

"Nothing wrong with my shit, okay! But I don't want to have sex every day."

"Because you can't fuck every day!" Biyell retorted. "Nigga got the nerve to have two bitches and one broke dick."

That's when I got concerned. "Telly, when do you turn forty?" I asked.

"Next month."

"Have you ever had a prostate exam?"

"Is that when the doctor lifts up your nut sack and says *caught*?" he asked.

"No nigga, it's when the doctor sticks his finger in your ass!" Jarvis said.

"For what?" Telly stopped smoking for the first time that night. "What does sticking a finger in my ass have to do with my dick going soft?"

"That's how they examine your prostate gland; they stick a

finger in your ass during the exam," I explained.

"Fuck that, Uncle Glenn!"

"So you're admitting something is going wrong?" Biyell asked. "Like you're really having issues?"

Telly was a little hesitant at first to answer, but finally said, "Sometimes, but she plays with it a little while; it gets hard again. Problem solved, yah heard me?"

"Telly, you need to set an appointment to have a full check-up with a prostate exam."

"Ain't nobody sticking a finger in my ass. If he can't examine that prostate no other way then fuck it. Guess I'll be pushing soft dick in her until it gets hard. Fuck that! I don't play that finger-in-asshole game. Niggas don't come back from that."

"Telly, what the fuck are you talking about?" Jarvis asked.

"That's why we have so many gay dudes walking around this city—went to the doctor and got poked in the ass, came home gay. Fuck you and that gay-ass doctor. Who's next on the game?"

And now you know why Madden Night is so important to these men; it's not so much about the game as it is about the things we can't say to anyone else. Even though we roast the fuck out of each other, our secrets never leave these four walls. We are a band of unlikely brothers from several different backgrounds with three common interests: Weed, women, and who's next on *Madden*. But all jokes aside, who knew Telly didn't know where the prostate was located? And who knew and Jarvis was willing to risk everything because Bri-Bri swallowed?

Who knew?

See you next Thursday.

CHAPTER 5

11:05 p.m.

JARVIS

I heard Uncle Glenn both times he asked the question, but I tried my best to ignore him. He doesn't understand what it feels like to have one of these—and getting one doesn't happen that often. Bri-Bri could wake up in the morning and decide she's had her fill, so in the meantime, I think it's in my best interest to get as much as she's willing to give. It's just sex, right? It's not like we're playing with real feelings; it's not like love. It's just sex between two consenting adults, and we're only related through marriage. Technically, we're strangers.

If Monica catches us together, could I do Briana for the rest of my life?

It's a real-time question.

I'm not sure.

Here's what I know for sure: I feel alive again after being sexually unconscious. It was Briana who gave me *mouth-to-dick* resuscitation. If she's capable of making me feel this way after one week, just imagine if I could enjoy her every day? Full time? I sound crazy—I know I do—but a passionless marriage is also bat-shit crazy. Don't I deserve a little pleasure in life other than one night out a week with the boys? Aren't I a good man?

Yes I am: a damn good man.

Married to the same *grouchy-ass* woman since college—my high school sweetheart, with the prom pictures to prove it. We built a life together, dreamed together, and grew into adults. I even watched her career skyrocket; never once gave her dissension about being the breadwinner, even though my self-esteem suffered through day-to-day starvation. So, I turned to writing. Writing became a place I could escape from her success without leaving the marriage; where I could feel a sense of accomplishment, where I mattered just as much as she mattered to me.

It felt like we were at the mall of life but on opposite sides of the escalator; she looked forward to the next level while I sauntered through the bargain basement.

With every promotion Monica received, one of my vital organs died—not due to jealousy, but regret. I've always loved the intoxicating effect of prose; my infatuation with words could, in fact, be my downfall. Monica always loved numbers. My wife became a banker while I, regrettably, settled for stacks of term papers in a classroom with chipped ceiling paint and a broken steam radiator. Monica begged me to major in finance with her and went to great lengths to map out the life we could have in Chicago or New York as portfolio managers, but I was possessive of my dream to one day watch my characters on the big screen. Maybe I should have fallen in love with numbers—she would have respected me more, perhaps?

The came euphoria from the most unlikely soul: Briana.

I have not felt like this since the first night I made love to Monica, which was also my first time making love, and that was forever ago. That's what this feeling is—I like how much Bri likes me. I like being liked. Love is overrated. Love is entrapping. Monica loves me, but it feels like shit. Bri likes me and it feels like *haaaaaah*. I want to be liked. I want a woman to be with me because she likes me—like is also freedom to unlike. I have no doubt that my wife loves me, but I know she doesn't like me. The good news is: Briana does.

I like that.

The warm smile in her voice when I call her sounds like she's waited in total darkness for my voice, then all of a sudden—*click*! The enthusiasm she has for me is the reason I am sitting here at her gated apartment complex. I'm waiting on this pizza delivery guy to open the gate or get the fuck out of the way. I'm in a hurry.

Bri-Bri is waiting for me.

She likes me.

She sent me a picture while I was losing to cheating-ass Timothy. A picture of a candlelit room. A picture she snapped from chin to toes. A black lace pair of panties.

Up ahead, the pizza guy just pissed me off. I exited my car and interrupted his speaker call through the security phone.

"Hey buddy, I am in a bit of a hurry. How about I punch in the code so you can drive through?" I didn't give him a chance to respond. I punched in 1215 on the dial pad. After a loud tone, the gate opened.

With the pizza guy out of the way, I drove through the security gate. With each speed bump, my dick grew harder than the chrome lock on a seatbelt. I knew she was waiting. She gave me my own code to the security gate and made the code my birthday because she was waiting. She came to see me at work the other day, sucked me off in my classroom, then gave me a key to her apartment. Now she's waiting. The security gate has already notified her that I'm twenty-two seconds from parking, and I know she's waiting.

I parked.

I inserted the key.

I followed the rose pedals to her bedroom.

I froze just inside the door to appreciate the sexiest woman I have ever kissed.

There she was, face-down on a pillow, black satin panties lifted as high as she could arch her back. There were four fingers hidden in those black panties. The moans, the scented candles, her skin shining like buttered dinner rolls right out the oven . . . she looked like a young Chilli from the girl group TLC if Chilli ever wanted to fuck me. *This has to be a dream.* Maybe I am stuck in one of my novels? Is this real? Is she real? I think she's lived another life. *How does she know how to stimulate me?*

"Hi baby," she said in a winded voice.

"Hi Bri . . ."

"Are you hungry?"

"No . . ."

"I could fix you something if you're hungry, I don't mind."

"I only want you." I unbuttoned my shirt and pants.

"But you have me."

"I do?"

"Yes, anytime you want me, you can have me." Her back started to buck from convulsions. Her ass cheeks clutched then released, then clutched again as she held her face buried in the pillow. The convulsions lasted for almost a minute, followed by a deep sigh of relief.

"Happy I was able to help, guess I can turn around and leave now," I teased.

"That's what you do to me." Her breathing was heavy; the room was humid, golden, and sticky. "I have always fantasized about you. In fact, the first time I made myself tremble, it was over a thought of you." Her eyes batted as she swayed those black panties from side to side.

"Did I cross your mind today?" I asked.

"Seriously, you couldn't tell?"

"Well I didn't want to assume."

"The lunchtime picture with the wet fingers wasn't convincing enough?"

It was, but I wanted to hear her say it.

"You were all I thought about," she crooned.

I wanted to dive on her, but then again I wanted to watch her. This was the image men beat their dicks to in prison. This was the image rich men enjoyed every night. This was the kind of woman I fantasized about as I walked the halls at work, peeking into classroom after classroom in search of the teacher babe of the day.

"So what did you think about?" she asked me.

"Are you going to wake up in the morning and lose your appetite for me? Is this just a thrill for you? Is it me, or is this a power-trip?"

She rolled to her side like a centerfold and pondered for a minute. "Since I was thirteen, men have tried to get me in bed. The ones who tried their best to conceal their lustful intent still gave themselves away with their eyes. But not you. At family events, your eyes never left my eyes, and I have never felt your eyes on my ass. Men always touch my ass with their eyes, but not you."

She has an ass that doesn't quit, and she knows it.

"You were always interested in me as a person. You asked me about my day, and my job, and about how it felt to be me in this crazy world. You talked to me about current things, and deep things. You are the only man to stimulate my mind. You are everything!"

I looked over my shoulder to see if someone else was standing behind me.

"Jarvis, I may be younger than you, but make no mistake—I am all woman, and you're not here by coincidence. I knew at the end of the Zulu Ball last year that you would be here tonight."

It was only then that she sat up in the bed, her back resting against the black, tufted headboard. "Open that closet?"

I did as I was told and opened the closet. Immediately, I was caught off guard by several men's shirts and pants—expensive clothes. On the floor were two pairs of men's shoes. *What kind of games is she playing with me? If she has a man, then why invite me in here?* I suddenly felt a strong since of panic, and a deflating feeling in my dick.

"Men's clothes, Briana? You have a man? But you never mentioned a guy . . ."

"That's because those clothes are for you," she smirked and pointed. "You wear a size eighteen neck, forty-two, thirty-two in pants, and size thirteen Allen Edmond shoes. For a year, I have been buying clothes for you because I knew one day you would stand in that closet."

The clothes still had their dangling tags. The receipts in the pockets of the pants and shoes were dated last year.

I don't remember how I made it from the closet to her lips. Maybe I hopped like Uncle Glenn? Maybe I crawled? Maybe I vaporized and then regenerated like Star Trek? How I arrived didn't matter—I had to kiss Briana. I had to suck her tongue. I had to bite her neck. I had to force all of me deep inside her walls, to feel her separate around me and hold me with the inner most part of her soul.

Her words oozed between my lips. "In each dresser drawer are undershirts for you, and boxers, and cologne. In the bathroom there's a new toothbrush, and on the back of the door there's a new robe. It's all for you. I am all for you. I waited for you."

Interlude.

"Jarvis?"

"Yes?"

"Do you think you could love me?"

"Of course I can."

"Not just my body . . . but me?" she placed my hand on her heart.

"Bri, yesterday I talked to you on and off for ten hours. I feel myself about to fall deeply in love with you."

"Do you want to fall?"

"Yes."

"Then you wouldn't mind if I gave you a little push."

Bri slipped out from under me and slid out of the bed. A seductive finger invited me to the sofa—I followed. She pulled down my boxers. I stepped out of them, then she pushed me down on the sofa. Then she took me in her mouth. I don't remember how long it took, but I do remember how I felt when it happened. It was spiritual. I left my body and watched from across the room as Briana sucked every ounce of reluctance out of my body. Suddenly I was pulled through a wormhole—everything went black, the universe opened, and I raptured. That unknown thing became known, and the answer was resounding.

Could I do Bri-Bri for life?

Fucking right!

CHAPTER 6

Madden Night
Thursday, March 9, 2017
6:03 p.m.

It's rare for the guys to arrive on time, but every purple moon it happens. Today it felt as if all five of them parked a block away from my house, and then, like stalkers, waited until Diana backed out of the parking lot. *I wonder if they were stalking the house?* I shook my head and shrugged. The reason they arrived every week wasn't as important as the fact that they arrived every single week—and I needed them just as much as they needed me.

In the days following my accident in the porta potty, my biggest fear was falling out of life. Like those poor Vietnam vets who returned home minus their cognitive abilities and a leg, confined to a rolling penitentiary that was more wheel than it was chair, I was prepared to roll down the same road—disabled from the waist down and giving *zero fucks* from the neck up. After my lower leg was painlessly removed, I was damn sure that was my fate. I sat in that wheelchair for the first time and said to

God, *give me death.*

Life for me came in the form of Diana and these five young men—these five imperfect brothers who would rather hang out with an imperfect dude like me when they could travel the world, attend a Super Bowl without pre-planning ramps, or take a swamp tour without worrying about how the crippled guy was going to board the scampers. Paradoxically, they chose me, and I prefer their company. Though I spend most of my time in this apartment, through their lives, I'm omnipresent.

I live.

I touch.

I breathe.

I stroll through the intricate details of their daily lives as they meander out and about in a world I'd never thought to miss, but still get to indulge in. They might have full use of all fingers and toes, but I have something they lack—eyes for one woman. I want that for them. I want them to enjoy this peace, this bliss, this feeling of total satisfaction, this plate of food that's so mouth-watering, I'm full, and I want these young brothers to experience what it feels like to exist in a state of universal contentment, assured that the woman they chose is just as capable of fulfilling their every desire—even inclinations and fancies not yet conceived in their restless minds. Convinced, as I'm convinced in Diana, that anything I desire is just a conversation away.

Ask, and you may receive.

If the way to a man's heart is through his stomach, then the way to a woman's hearts is through security. Somehow, I must get these brothers to see that juggling multiple women is no way to live when the right woman can give you the world. And I'm not naïve—I don't believe that all marriages were meant to be, divorce court proves that every day—but some of these men are throwing away perfectly good women chasing a person who doesn't exist. I remember when my dad once said: *He who cometh to his woman must first believe that she is his woman and is a rewarder of a man who diligently seeks her.*

If only I could convince these brothers to focus on one woman—those beautiful wives who have pledged allegiance to their happiness. If only they would listen to me, that would allay that unquenchable fire, that much I know for sure.

I also know each one of them.

I've developed individual relationships with all of them, so I know the other side of them that they hide from the group. I also know each one of them is a conductor of his own little hoe train filled with oblivious passengers—unknowing women who will suffer catastrophic injuries after the derailment, ejected because of the guys' whorish tendencies.

Take for instance, Timothy. Today he isn't smoking—that's how I know something is wrong. Timothy loves weed more than food. Yet there he is, sitting there with a mound of weed on the coffee table gazing straight ahead, pretending to be here. I guess anywhere is better than home.

"Timothy, what's up with you today?"

"Nothing, Uncle Glenn, just chilling."

"What's up with you and Tootsie? You haven't mentioned her lately."

We still don't know her real name, but his wife's name is Kayla.

"We're good; she was at my studio yesterday. She needed a few head shots."

"I bet she did!" Biyell called over the voice of Lil Wayne.

Timothy is one of those African American brothers so light in complexion he could be easily mistaken for Puerto Rican. He's also bulky like an American Samoan. Unlike Rasta, who just lets his hair do whatever the fuck it wants to do, Timothy is razor-shaven and trimmed. He's married, but never mentions his wife unless it's to complain about her weight or her snooping through his things. According to Timothy's description, Kayla is tall and used to be runway thin, but due to a thyroid issue and a new location of Café Dauphine opening on the next block, she's put on a few extra pounds. If you let Timothy tell it, she looks like two offensive linemen standing side-by-side. Trust me on this one, it was only a few extra pounds, but Timothy is also the most dramatic out of the five, and the one who derails the most.

"How long has it been now with you and Tootsie?" I asked.

"It's been about two months."

"How's the *pussssay?*" I knew Biyell was going to ask. Then Rasta hyped him up—then came another freestyle rap about pussy.

"Did you eat that pusssay, did you beat that pusssay, did you sleep in that pusssssay? Three-piece that pusssssssssssssssay?!" Biyell free-styled.

Tim shook his head. "I really don't know, haven't gotten there yet."

Every face in the room frowned at Timothy as if he'd farted during communion.

"What are you waiting for, marriage? You're married already!" Jarvis said.

"I'm taking my time with this one, slowing it down a little."

"Nigga, please! Get the fuck out of here. What's really going on?" Telly fussed. "Women don't wait two months to fuck anymore because they're too afraid to lose out to a quick-pussy bitch. So if she hasn't fucked you yet . . . something is wrong with you or something is wrong with her."

"It's not me, but then again, it is."

"Told y'all," Telly said.

"She has a man, so that's why I haven't pushed the sex issue, and the other part is . . . I want Tootsie all to myself."

"Say what? She's married?" Biyell asked. "I love married women. They never call your phone in the middle of the night. They never pop up unannounced, and married women are perfectly fine with just fucking you. They love having variety dick. Take my advice, leave these single women alone. Target the married women."

"Thank you for the PSA on married pussy, but she's not married, she has a man." Timothy went on to explain, "Tootsie is, she's just . . . different. She's not happy with her man, and I'm miserable with my so-called wife."

"There you go with that *so-called* bullshit, with your whiny ass!" I got angry.

"So I get it, you two are planning a prison break," Telly gathered.

"For lack of a better term, I'm ready to divorce Kayla."

Telly got excited. "HELLO! I'm running a divorce special right now—$695 down and $695 when we get to court. I could have you *free* like the Ohio Players before the five o'clock news," Telly pitched.

"Hold the fuck up!" I leaped from my bar stool. "I know you're not about to divorce Kayla because she gained weight?"

Biyell paused the game. "You have a problem with thick girls? You're cutting her loose because she's thick?"

"She's fat," Timothy corrected him.

"Mutha-fucker, you fat—DJ Khaled-looking-ass nigga!" Biyell took offense. "Thick women are the best thing God created—"

Tim cut him off. "God didn't make her fat; she made herself fat."

"Tim, go fly two kites! She gained a few pounds, it happens! Women are like your 401k; you can't pull everything out at the first sign of trouble. You have to be in it for the long haul. If the pussy's still good and she's still beautiful and treats you good, love every inch of her," Biyell advised.

"Nigga, you like 'em big because they're easy to catch!" Timothy addressed Biyell.

I know it's a figure of speech, but I really heard a needle drag across a record. The other brothers knew what was coming. Some of them tried to look away, but it was too late.

"Bruh, what you are trying to say?" Biyell tensed up.

"Dude, I'm saying, in three years I have never seen you with a woman any of us would date. So it's either you're too afraid to

approach a smaller woman, or that weak-ass game you're shooting only works on *fat chicks*."

Everybody stood up. A line had been crossed. The last time a
line was crossed, it took an hour to separate Timothy and Telly.

"Number first of all, nigga, I don't fuck with skinny women
because I don't feel like kissing a bitch's ass for two months . . .
for two dollars' worth of pussy. The other reason you like skinny
women is because you're kicking stomach down the street. How
da-fuck you want a skinny wife, but you can't lose weight?"
Rasta and Jarvis held Biyell back. "Let me go, bruh; we're just
talking."

"Yeah, let the nigga go!" Timothy held his dukes up high.

"Everybody chill out, all right? Timothy has made up his
mind to divorce Kayla, and all of you need to mind your business." Telly tried to calm the room by lowering his voice to a
whisper. "You've never been to my new office, but here's my
card. I can meet with you any time after four!"

Jarvis took offense. "Telly, this ain't the time to be passing out
cards for divorces—we're trying to work through this."

"Coming from the nigga who's still fucking his niece? Here's
a card for you too, because Monica will catch your ass."

"Tim-Tim, my man, don't listen to Telly—he knows you have
cash, and he's broke," Rasta intervened. "Take it from me, stay
out of court. Y'all know Telly is my lawyer and I love him, but
what's not written on his card is those judges at the civil court
are all black women. They hate men—all men. During my divorce proceedings, Telly couldn't get a word in—I thought the
judge was going to slap the piss out of him when he tried to
object. I was $9,500 in arrears when we left the court; ordered
to pay $950 a month. Trust me, Tim-Tim, stay the fuck out of
court."

Timothy's face turned as red as Ragu sauce. "Then what am
I supposed to do? Huh? Should I live the rest of my life with a
woman I no longer find attractive? When I'm seventy-five years
old, will I get a trophy for that? A standing ovation in church

for hanging in there with the wrong woman? Think about what you're suggesting."

"But Tim, you stood before God and made a vow for better or for worse, which also includes fat or skinny! You can't quit her like an online date gone wrong. You have to remember your vows to God, at least," I tried to appeal to his sense of decency.

"True—during our wedding ceremony, we stood before God. When Rasta got married, he stood before God. But when Rasta's wife left him because of his bootleg religion—"

Rasta objected to his feet and removed the netted cap that contained his dreadlocks. His dreads slithered across his head like eight black snakes. "Show some RESPECT for the Emperor *Haile Selassie* born Tafari Makonnen Woldemikael who was King of Kings and ruler of Ethiopia . . ." he recited Rastafarian litanies.

Tim cut Rasta off. "Dude, *shhhhhh* with that shit. Please! The point I'm making is when ole girl decided she didn't want a Rastafarian husband, did she go back to God and ask him for a divorce?"

I didn't have an answer. Neither did anyone else.

"Did she go back to the same altar and ask God to free her from that nappy-head nigga over there?"

"Nappy head nigga?! Hold up. Hold up. Who you calling a nappy-head nigga?"

"Did I stutter?" Timothy confirmed.

Rasta stepped across the coffee table, causing Jarvis and Telly to form a roadblock on the other side. Ever true to form, Timothy had just crossed another line, and now things were spinning out of control fast.

"Just hear me out," Timothy's arms extended straight forward. "When it was time to say *I do*, they stood before God, but when it was time to say *I don't*, they stood in front of a judge. How could a judge end something that was declared *holy* by God? I don't want to hear shit about marriage vows."

The only voice heard after Timothy spoke was that of Jay-Z.

Timothy made good use of the silence to drive home his point. "If Tammy could leave Rasta over hair and weed, why am I the worst nigga on the planet if I leave Kayla because she gained ninety-five pounds?"

"Timothy, I know you're frustrated with her weight, but come on brother, slow your roll for a second. Have you considered working out with her?" I asked.

"And if I said no?"

"I'm just saying; maybe if you two start working out together, then she'll feel better about losing weight?"

"Uncle Glenn, the reason my wife gained weight is because she got comfortable. That's what they do; when they're single and have to compete against other bitches for our attention, everything is tight and light, but once they hook you, they say *fuck it*. When I married her, I did not waive my right to a preference. I prefer her the way she was!" Timothy lit his blunt for the first time tonight.

"Y'all niggas tripping in here!" Biyell said. "Done blew a good high!"

"My final point," Tim said in an exasperated tone, "is women have the right to leave us if we cheat, but she can blow up to four hundred pounds and I can't say shit? Fuck that! The reason she gained that weight is because she no longer gives a fuck about what I think, what I like, or what I find attractive and sexy. But if she catches me looking at a woman the size she used to be—then she tries to square up. Telly, I will see you Monday at four p.m. I'm out!" Timothy dropped the controller and puffed his way out.

"Real question, what just happened?" Jarvis asked.

"Y'all niggas trippin!" Biyell replied.

"Let Timothy walk it off, I'll call him tomorrow," I said.

"Those female judges in New Orleans Civil Court hate black men more than the Klan—watch how bad they lynch his ass," Rasta shook his head.

"Have any of you ever met Kayla?" Jarvis asked. "I haven't."

None of us had ever met Timothy's wife.

"He can jump stupid and let her go; imma scoop her up at divorce court!" Biyell laughed. "Who got winners?"

CHAPTER 7

Five minutes later

Timothy was upset—the screeching of his tires out of the parking lot confirmed it—but there was still a lot of weed to smoke and many *Madden* games to play. With each puff, I could tell Timothy's words still echoed, because the remaining guys took long, hard drags, but not much was said. Despite the two altercations in one night, Rasta was still on pace to roll our weekly love offering of blunts. When he's focused, it's common for him to roll thirty blunts in thirty-minutes. Tonight we had nineteen.

Damn you Timothy, for distracting Rasta.

But I could understand Timothy's point even if I disagreed with him; women divorce us for every reason under the sun and it's never frowned upon, but when we divorce them for being overweight, then we're the worst pieces of shit to ever step foot in a courtroom. Take, for instance, my cousin Pootie: His wife blew up so big she was declared disabled and he never said a word. He protested with his feet. I'm not saying he was right, but Belinda was a stay-at-home wife!

On the other hand, I felt Pootie could have at least given her a warning—dude came home and heard her snoring from the front porch, got back in his car, and never returned. I'm not exaggerating—he didn't even pack a pair of drawls, and he never mentioned another word about Belinda. She later died in her sleep, and it was then that we discovered that sneaky bastard had her loaded down in insurance. He then married a yoga instructor name Mimi. When I last saw him at his son's wedding, Pootie was happier than a punk with a sack of dicks. Now back to Timothy.

That little primadonna had raised a good question: do men waive their rights to a physical preference once we say *I do*? On this Madden Night, that was the question presented to us, and it a question only one was bold enough to answer. Whereas Timothy hated big girls, Biyell never saw one he could resist. He could find something fuckable in any woman no matter the size, shape, or color. Biyell was truly an Equal Opportunity Dicksman.

"Biyell, help me understand something . . ."

Just as I was about to ask him to explain his theory on BBWs, he shushed me with a finger. Then his hand covered his mouth. His eyes stretched to max capacity. A picture on his phone had induced an anxiety attack. He crept to the window and softly peeked through my blinds, through the V-shaped section in the middle that was bent by Jarvis.

"*Fuck! Fuck! Fuck! She's outside!*" Biyell about-faced from the window. He paced from the entertainment center to the kitchen counter and back again. "She figured it out. *Fuck, Fuck, Fuck!*"

"Figured what out?" Jarvis asked.

"Who's outside?" Telly asked.

Before Biyell could answer, Jarvis ran to the window.

"B, isn't that your wife outside?"

"*Fuck! Fuck! Fuck!*" Biyell's panic level was full-blown.

"If Tamera is outside, then invite her in," I said.

"No, no, no, not tonight!" Biyell replied frantically.

"Then bring her a plate . . ." I suggested.

"Hell no! Not going out there."

"Why not?"

"I think she may have caught me."

"Oh no," I said.

"Hold up! You scared?" Rasta was amused. "Not big *bad-ass* Biyell! Not Mr. Hot Boy! I know you're scared to go outside and remind your wife who's the boss!" Rasta finally got the chance to lay into Biyell. "Not Big Pimpin'. Not the dude who said married women don't pop up unannounced—Tamera did."

"Fuck you Rasta, I have a crisis going on."

"Fellas, did any of you know Tamera was coming here tonight?" No one replied. "Looks like she has rolled up on your ass to me." Rasta choked on the weed smoke. "Bruh, what did you do?"

By this point, all of us were peeking through my window like the police had just kicked in my neighbor's door. Every time we tried to get to the bottom of why Tamera was outside in the parking lot, we could only manage to get one word out of Biyell.

Fuck!

"Biyell what did you do? We may be able to help you get through this, but you have to come clean. What did you do?" I asked.

On his final rotation from the window, Biyell continued to the kitchen. Like a pine tree, dude was motionless. He stared at the ceiling in search of a way out of a trap; a trap that was set by his wife. Biyell was busted—Tamera's headlights illuminating my living room left little doubt—but what did he do to piss her off? That part was still unclear.

"Biyell, brother, talk to me—what did you do?" I asked again as Jarvis woke his laptop from a deep sleep and we all heard that familiar clicking sound.

After five minutes ticked away on my microwave clock, Biyell recovered from his sudden case of laryngitis. He finally spoke.

"Well, Uncle Glenn, it all started early this morning when . . ."

CHAPTER 8

Madden Thursday
March 9, 2017
2:15 a.m.

TAMERA

I sleep better when we spoon throughout the night; it's the reason I wrap my hair in silk, just to feel the rhythm of his breath on the thin of my neck. I toss and turn without the security that comes from being constricted against his body—prodded every other hour by his manhood in the center of my back, groped like a crowded bus ride. The air above my bed is thick with testosterone and before dawn, it will fall like the dew. What's his is his. Even unconscious, that includes me. Nevertheless, I surrender. Even though he wakes me up at least a handful of times every night, I awaken even more often when he's working nights out of town. It is what it is: a miracle that I get any sleep at all.

But what has me awake at this hour of night is not the bulk of his arm, or his vibrating snore, or his callous cuff of my breast—

not it the least. There's something more precious than a snooze, more rejuvenating than a nap—only the truth could provide me a peaceful sleep tonight.

The first challenge to sneaking out of bed is to free myself from his bulk. Then, I can twinkle my toes into my slippers. This is the perfect hour to liberate myself.

On his side of the bed, on the nightstand, is his cell phone, and I can't sleep because of this nagging hunch. I know it's not right to go through his phone, but something is troubling me in my spirit, and I feel like the Lord woke me for this reason. Who am I to ignore the voice of the Lord when he says *wake up and check your husband's cell phone*?

He's God, and I should obey.

Agree?

The truth is I have never caught my husband cheating—not once in the ten years since we jumped the broom. Sure, I've had to check him about a "like" queen on Facebook who commented on all his posts, with little hearts and laughing emojis as if Biyell were funnier than Richard Pryor, but other than that, I have never caught him in the act. And no woman has ever knocked on my door informing me about *this or that* concerning my husband as if my well-being were her utmost concern. I have never experienced any of that . . . so why am I in the bathroom at 2:22 a.m. trying to crack the log-in code to his cell phone? Because the Lord told me to check his cell phone.

A true story.

I've tried his birthday, my birthday, his mom's birthday, our daughter's birthday, and his grandmother's birthday, but it's still locked. I only have another thirty minutes or so before he wakes up to pee. It's always around the same time: 3:00 a.m. to 3:15 a.m. *I'm still locked out.* Why do I feel like he's cheating on me when I know his whereabouts every minute of the day? When he's away for work, he still texts me back pretty quickly when I check in, unless he's asleep. The only time he goes out is on Thursday, to play that stupid football game by Uncle Glenn.

Go figure, a bunch of grown men playing a video game every week—how childish. If I didn't put my foot down, he wouldn't come home until after midnight, talking about, *Baaaybay, I'm in first place at the tournament I'll be home a little later.*

Like hell you will!

When he joined that *Madden Football* club I made him send me pictures every thirty minutes just to make sure he was at Uncle Glenn's house—and he was.

So why do I feel like he's cheating on me? This is crazy, but I can't escape this feeling. I constantly hear that little voice in the back of my head: *Don't sabotage our happiness.* This should be our happy time. I should feel secure. I finally got my degree and can take some of the financial load off my husband—just in time, too. For the past two years his checks have been short about eight hundred dollars a month. So, the little voice says I should just chill and enjoy the moment . . . but then there's another voice going off like a smoke alarm!

Why is his cell phone password-protected from me?

Why don't we share any passwords?

Why is it I have a debit card to his checking account, but I never see any statements? Why is it that every time I ask him to add me, he comes up with a work excuse?

See, see, what had happened was . . . we were supposed to go to the bank today, but I got stuck on a job.

Oh what a convenient excuse that is—it gets him out of everything. *I got stuck on a job.* Maybe I'm just paranoid, but there's only one way to know, and that's to know. Today on my Rosetta Stone app it said *Doveryai, no proveryai* in Russian; that means *Trust, but verify.* I trust my husband, but I need to verify.

My God, this is aggravating!

What's the combination?

Our anniversary?

I can still remember it like yesterday. My girlfriend had just moved into her new condo, and she asked me to house-sit for the cable man while she ran to the hardware store. Honey, let me tell you, I was sitting on the loveseat minding my business on Face-book, then he knocked on the door. So I opened that door. I was expecting him, but I wasn't expecting that—I mean him—Bi-yell. Normally when you think *the cable man,* a guy who looks eight months pregnant with musty armpits comes to mind, but the complete opposite knocked on the door.

My eyes started right inside his flashing eyes, then quickly darted down along his jaw and shoulder blades. They took in the lines of his body and lingered for a long second around his belt buckle.

I'm lying.

My eyes soaked in his shape, his muscle, his hungry smile.

I'm lying.

My eyes slowly scanned every inch of his body like that red light in an MRI machine, flashing on high alert around the area where the dick lives. I think it was two minutes later when I finally came to. Then he spoke. His voice sounded like Barack Obama with an arm full of cable wire. I said, *Lord, you mean to tell me . . . all of this is for me?*

I'm lying.

I said, *this sundress is long, but if he keeps lookin' at me like that, we gonna Christian her condo today.* I think that's what I said, or I maybe said, *it would behoove me to fuck this cable man,* but I wasn't *saved and sanctified* at the time, therefore this confession is covered under the blood. Amen and glory to his name.

But I would've fucked him!

Oops, keep that on the low.

Then I discovered he was single, but I wasn't single at the time. When he announced he was single, though, I became sin-gle too. There was the little technicality of informing my ex, but later that evening I told Donovan it was over—*dude take it light.* That too is now covered with the blood.

Where was I? That's right . . .

Biyell was the sexiest man I'd ever stood close to, and I wanted him! And when did they start hiring models to install cable? His skin, his face, that deep-dimpled smile, those fluorescent teeth . . . and Biyell spoke with an astonishing degree of intellect. I said, *Lord, this is my husband*, and the Lord said, *eat up, my child*. If he had proposed right then and there, I would have said yes, gave him some on her sofa, and hopped in his cable truck.

Shaquanta would have been like, *Bitccch you left my front door wide open!* Shaquanta ain't saved; not even a penny's worth of Jesus in her. *Bitcccch I asked you to watch my house and you're gone?*

Gone with the cable man.

Three weeks later I was really gone.

I was so in love with Biyell that on my days off, I would ride in the truck with him and lick my lips while he climbed from one roof to the next. After he snapped on his tool belt, he grabbed a huge ladder in one arm and a big spool of cable wire in the other and carried them from the truck to the side of the house. All day, every day. That explained his body. *My God, that body.*

I remember the first time we made love; everything was going about normal until he started sweating like the black cop on the TV show *In the Heat of the Night*. Then he did something no man had done since I was a teenager . . . he picked me up! I started speaking in tongues.

Jesus-is-comin-in-a-Honda-leavin-in-a-Chevrolet.

Biyell picked me up and sat *all of this* woman on the dresser. I felt him. He was deep. For nearly two hours he reached areas in me I didn't know a penis could go—he gave me the kinds of orgasms I never even knew existed until he made his way inside. That was it for me. We married three months later, and I could still feel the first time he touched me. *Jesus Jaquan Christ, that's it.*

I know how to break into this phone!

Why didn't I think of that earlier?

It's 2:48 a.m.

Sometimes he opens his phone with a code and other times he touches it with his index finger. And since he's snoring, and his hands are free, I'll simply borrow his index finger. I tip-toed back to my side of the bed, lifted his right finger, and pressed it against the glass surface of his phone, but nothing happened. Then I remembered—Biyell is left-handed.

I pressed the index finger on his left hand against the finger-print recognition and I heard the greatest sound ever.

Shwinnnnnnng!

I'm in!

Let's start with the pictures . . .

CHAPTER 9

Madden Night
9:45 p.m.

He spoke in incoherent riddles intertwined with complete gibberish. For a moment I wondered if he was catching a stroke—the symptoms were about the same. It was once said that *anticipation of death is actually worse than death*: never had there been a more accurate description of Biyell. We tried to get Biyell to calm down, but all attempts failed. Tamera was outside, he was inside, and somewhere in between was the truth. Judging from the way he continued to stare at my kitchen ceiling and the picture on his phone, I concluded that some lady on his installation route had gifted Biyell a nude photo. Boy was I wrong.

Telly tried to get him to open up. "Dude I'm a lawyer. I make my living helping people get out of tight situations, but I can't help you unless you open up."

With those words, Telly made a breakthrough. After a deep breath, Biyell began to speak.

"It was about three in the morning when I thought I heard my phone power up . . ."

After that first sentence, I started to pray for Biyell. *Dear Lord, I come to you as your humble servant.*

Biyell continued, "I didn't think much of it, but I had to pee, so I headed to the bathroom. When I opened the door, Tamera was sitting on the toilet with my phone."

We need you right now, Lord.

"Dude, how did she hack into your phone?"

"I don't fucking know! I have a lock on it, but somehow she cracked it."

"Please tell me you didn't have pictures of women from your install route?" Telly asked.

"Hell no, I don't keep pictures, I delete all texts. I don't even have pictures of my kids in my phone because I delete everything at the end of every day."

"Apparently she found something, because that white Escalade ain't moving," Jarvis's messy ass waved at Tamera, and she waved back. "Nice rims, by the way."

"Jarvis, get cho-ass out that window—she can see you!" Biyell freaked out.

"Listen to me, Potty Dick, even if I close the curtains, *Tamera* knows you're here," Jarvis reminded him.

Rasta joined Jarvis in the window. "Yeah, she's sitting nice—those factory rims?"

"Bruh, fuck those rims! Jarvis get out of the window!" Biyell snapped.

"Dude, your car is outside, and she's parked tight against your door so you can't open it. You're done—go outside and face her," Jarvis prompted.

"Jarvis, mind your fuckin' business!" Biyell snapped.

"This is my only night out a week . . . this is my business!" Jarvis laughed

"This shit ain't funny, fuck you."

"Here's what I don't understand," Telly tried to process Biyell's situation. "If there were no picture of bitches in your phone and no text messages, I don't see what the problem is."

"The problem is I had a picture of my dick in the phone."

"Okay, what's the problem with that? It's your phone. It's your dick. Case closed," Telly shrugged.

"Because I never sent her that picture of my dick!"

"Oh, oh!" Jarvis said.

"Rule number 327-14, section four: *If you plan to do anything special for your mistress, make sure you do double for your wife!* Send the same dick picture to your wife, and you avoid suspicion should she flip through your phone," Telly recited from the code book.

"I know! I know! And normally I would have, but my daughter can reach the damn doorknobs now, and she almost caught me trying to take the picture of my dick."

"I'm high, but I think I follow you," Rasta said. "You got up to go take a piss, and she was on the toilet with your phone and a picture of your dick that you didn't send her. Then what happened?"

"Then she says, *I find it funny*—"

I cut him off. "Oh no, she led off with *I find it funny?* You was done right there!"

"*I find it funny there is a picture of your dick in your phone, but I never received this picture . . .*"

"How did you reply?" Telly asked while Jarvis banged away on his laptop.

"Yeah, what was your comeback?" Jarvis asked.

Across the room, Rasta paid Telly his retainer, then packed away the rest of his weed.

"I panicked, I freaked out!"

"What did you do?" Telly asked with great concern.

"Tamera asked me who I sent a picture of my dick to—I gave the worst answer any man could give."

"Bruh! Bruh! What the fuck did you say?!" Jarvis's fingers paused.

"I said, *that ain't my dick!*"

"*Nigga . . . what?!*" Rasta screamed from the living room.

"THAT AIN'T MY DICK?" Crowd Noise Telly repeated. "THAT AIN'T . . . MY DICK?"

I think I laughed so hard I fainted. Jarvis was in the process of drinking when he heard *That ain't my dick*, and water spat out the sides of his mouth like a garden hose. Rasta dropped a lit blunt on the carpet. When I came to, Telly was crawling from the kitchen to the front door, he couldn't stand up.

Rasta was somewhere under the coffee table choking and gasping for air. Behind me, Jarvis slid out of his chair down to the kitchen floor while Biyell screamed out, "*That shit ain't funny, dog, that shit ain't funny!*" It was funny as fuck!

Rasta was the first to recover. "So if it wasn't your dick, was it . . . my dick?"

"Mannn, mannn, fuck you, Rasta! You forgot *Shameka* threw your five pairs of drawls all over the parking lot. Nigga only got drawls for Monday through Friday," Biyell lashed out at Rasta.

"That may be true, but I never disowned my dick!" Rasta snapped back.

"Serious shit, B," Jarvis tried to regain control of the crisis. "We're just trying to close this investigation on the stolen dick in your phone. Is there a reward for that dick?"

"Laugh all you want, but I panicked. I always deny, deny, deny, but this time it came out wrong."

"But why deny it was your dick in your phone? Don't you hear how fucked up that sounds?" I tried to talk some sense into him.

"I know that, but I fuckin' panicked, okay?!"

From down the hall, we heard, "This nigga . . . this nigga . . . said . . . that ain't my...dick! Oh Lord, Lord, please! My stomach hurts!" Telly couldn't breathe; he was catching an asthma attack.

I finally composed myself enough to ask another question regarding the stolen dick picture in Biyell's phone. "Biyell, after you said it wasn't your dick . . . what did she say?"

"Well, Tamera looked at the phone, then stuck her hand through the fly part of my boxers and pulled out my dick. Then she placed the phone next to my dick. Looking up at me, she said, *Because I love you, I will give you a do-over on that question. Now sweetie, my little pumpkin pie, who did you send a picture of your dick to?*"

"Biyell, please tell me you told her the truth! If you said that wasn't your dick a second time, I will pick up this refrigerator and bust your fuckin' head, boy!" Jarvis threatened.

"I said, *That ain't my dick*," Biyell admitted.

Telly crawled over to the front door and reclined against it, doubled over in a silent laugh.

"She was like, *If they lined up a thousand dicks, I could identify yours in the dark. It appears you take me for a fool, but let me enlighten you. You say that's not your dick, and if that's your story, then you stick with it, because it may not be your dick in this photo, but that's my rug in the picture, and my shower curtain.*"

"Then what happened?" I asked.

"Then she stood up and said, Before ten o'clock tonight, *I will know who you sent a picture of your dick to.*"

"What time is it, Rasta?" Jarvis hollered.

"It's 9:59 p.m. . . *Do you know where your dick is?*" Rasta asked in a deep baritone.

"Mannn, fuck you, Rasta!" Biyell was pissed and afraid.

After about ten minutes of dragging him to the front door, Biyell eventually went out to face Tamera. Unlike Rasta, he was smart enough to have his confrontation in the car and not create a scene. Through the windshield of their Escalade, we watched her neck roll perfidiously as she spoke only inches from his nose. As for Biyell, he just sat there; sometimes he got in a word, other times he backhand-slapped one of his hands into the other as he tried to make his point. I'm not sure he had one.

As for me, all I could think about was, *Did Tamera just discover GiGi and Biyell's outside children; one in her belly, and a*

daughter the same age as her daughter?
    I will let you know next Thursday.

CHAPTER 10

Madden Thursday
March 16, 2017
7:37 a.m.

I love to cook; if I had to do it all over again, I would've never answered that ad for the railroad and followed my heart. My heart is in the kitchen of a restaurant with my name in neon lights:

Eat at Glenn's.

It's the second biggest regret I have—that I never gave my dreams a chance. It's one thing when someone says you're not good enough, but when you say it to yourself? That is just as deadly as putting a gun to your temple and pulling the trigger. And sometimes you can put the gun to your head, pull the trigger, smell the smoke from the discharged bullet, and still live. That's what I did to myself; I killed my dreams.

I have always found it fascinating how perfectly green the grass is in cemeteries; how just below the soil lies the finality of so many hopes and dreams. Flowers still grow in the cemetery, and butterflies still rest on their petals.

At this stage in my life, there are two things that I'm passionate about:

Diana!

Goals!

I think that's the reason I cling onto my five *Madden Football* buddies, even in their unsettled states: they all have goals. They all are chasing a dream in their own way. They inspired me to chase my dream. Recently, I sat at this table and wrote a menu for my dream restaurant. Every day, I have cooked a meal from my menu, and my only customer has loved every dish. What a joy it is to cook for her.

This morning, after several failed attempts, I finally managed to carve two heart-shaped pancakes. Then I slumbered them on a mattress of fluffy golden eggs and topped them off with some fired apples. On the side of the plate are two thinly sliced strips of marinated steak, because Diana doesn't eat pork, but I do. On my plate are three strips of crispy bacon, because I find it blasphemous to eat pancakes without bacon. Hidden in her glass of orange juice this morning is a spoonful of gin, and the glass is placed next to a bowl of kiwi. On the side the kiwi, folded like a little tent, is a handwritten card scribed with my thoughts of the morning. I'm something like a poet on Thursday mornings, check out my flow:

Dear Diana, this morning I had a conversation with God and asked him for a favor. If I should die before you, then I ask that he send me back immediately, because my wife is my heaven. My paradise is making love to you and kissing you, and kissing you in the mornings. You are my heaven.

I know that probably sounds a little over-the-top, but it's easy to write poetry when you're in love. My soul loves my wife. When we first started out, when I was just a boyfriend and she was simply my girl, even I thought this feeling couldn't last. It had to be a phase. Surprisingly, my enamored feeling for Diana has outlasted every couple who married before us, even those who hated on us and said we would never make it a year. That was over two decades ago, and I still feel the way I felt on the day I realized we were no longer two separate parts, but a singular organism. A real couple.

Since that epiphany moment, I have never desired or thought of anyone else other than Diana. It's quite amazing considering we were never supposed to be. We were forbidden; what some would call . . . illicit. The front door just opened. I'll reveal more about that later. Diana has returned from her nightshift.

Before she made it midway down the hall, I hopped to the entertainment center and pressed play. Her favorite song.

"When I First Saw You" from the Broadway play *Dream Girls*.

Her slender frame veered in my direction. Even Ernie Barnes couldn't paint a more perfect smile. She tossed her purse on the sofa. Her sweater landed atop the lamp shade. Her keys landed in the abyss of the sofa cushions, hidden until it was time for her to leave again. But it didn't matter. Nothing mattered. Every care and concern from the past twelve hours was left in the back seat of her car. Diana was home.

"Why do you do this to me?" Her kisses were aggressive, the nibbles on my neck were painful and pleasurable. I sucked her tongue into my mouth and held it between my lips—it tasted like stale coffee, but I refused to let it go. There was a *pluck* sound when she managed to free her mouth.

"Your food is getting cold," I warned.

"That's why they made microwaves." She returned to her favorite area of my neck—right where it curves into my shoulder.

"Ouch! Ow-weee!"

"Stop whining," she bullied.

With both hands on her hips, I spun her. "Diana, do you see

those heart-shaped pancakes with the fried apples on top?"

"Yes," she replied in an airy voice.

"Seven pancakes had to die just to get two perfectly shaped hearts. Have a seat and eat your breakfast."

She turned with a long lip pout. "Okay . . . all right." She moseyed to her chair. I counted down as she sipped her spiked orange juice. "You have me so spoiled."

And just like she did yesterday, she reached for the folded card.

I started a mental countdown. *Ten, nine, eight, seven, six . . .*

My eyes followed her eyes across every sentence. Then, her eyes narrowed as her hand covered her lips. I knew what was coming—neck.

Five, four, three, two, one! I tried to hop away as fast as I could. Unfortunately, I only made it four hops into the living room before she tackled me near the sofa. She attacked the waistband of my pajama pants—I tried to stop her.

"Diana, eat your breakfast . . ." The tug of war for my pajama pants continued.

How did she get out of those scrub pants and work panties so quickly? From the waist up she was Nurse Diana Braxton—her ID badge was still clamped to her pocket. From the waist down she was butt-ass naked and wasn't taking no for an answer. I was pinned and mounted. For the next thirty minutes, she took what she wanted and how much she wanted until my dick was at zero percent charge; then she rolled off me. In that space between the sofa and the coffee table, she eventually dosed off, and then I dozed off.

We were out for about two hours when I heard the banging on the front door. I looked around for my pajama pants only to find them clotheslined across the television, where they hung on for dear life. I hopped across Diana, who was snoring like a chainsaw. Then came another bang on the door. I fell back on the lo-veseat, slid my leg into the pants, and made my way to the door.

In my Sam & Dave voice I called out, *"Hold on, I'm coming. Hold on, I'm coming."*

When I opened the door, it was the UPS guy; he knows about my leg.

"Good morning, Mr. Braxton."

"Good morning, Yonnis. What cha-got for me?"

"Just a signature-only package."

I grabbed the clipboard from Yonnis. "When are you coming to *fight your dog?* I am starting to think you're scared."

"You don't want these Cowboys, Mr. Braxton . . . you just think you do."

I signed his clipboard, and despite my best effort, my signa-ture still looked like the old Etch-a-Sketch game. "Well, you know what we do every Thursday night, and all of my dogs are killers! You bring those Cowboys, I promise you . . . we will chew 'em up!"

"Mr. Braxton, I'll see you tonight! Have your dogs ready!"

"Okay, but I'm letting you know right now—once you step foot in here, we're locking the door."

Yonnis laughed as he raced back to his truck. Once inside, he hit the horn twice. I hopped back to the living room with a large gold envelope only to find the woman who had sexually assault-ed me still on the floor, looking like somebody drugged her. I fell back on the loveseat and opened the envelope. It was from my lawyer—a settlement offer regarding my lawsuit. After reading it, I hopped over to my wife, and with soft fingers, I covered her face with the letters.

When she finally woke from her coma around noon, I was in the shower.

The bathroom door blew open: her face was a whirlwind of shock and awe.

"Glenn, nine million dollars? NINE MILLION FUCKING DOLLARS?!"

"That's nine million dollars should you choose to accept."

"You haven't called them to accept this?"

"No, because I wanted you to decide."

Diana placed the settlement letter from my attorney on the sink, removed her top, and inched her way into my shower. Under the warm water, we held each other. Our lives changed that morning.

After our shower, we returned to the kitchen and enjoyed our noonday breakfast.

What a perfect start to Madden Day.

CHAPTER 11

Madden Thursday
March 16, 2017
11:45 a.m.

TELLY

O f all the degrees offered at Southern University, why did I pick law? Why I did do this to my life? I fucking hate court. I hate these hard church pew benches, and I hate these broomstick-up-the-ass judges who only became judges because of dirty cash and ass-kissing campaigns. To say we're on the good side of the fence is a joke—everything about the judicial system is crooked and criminal. Just look around this civil court building, for instance: Most of the cases were decided in the judge's chambers during pre-trials, which are nothing more than *I-gave-you-something-now-give-me-something* shakedowns.

I fucking hate this place.

The guy next to me is Paul Stein, a pot-bellied attorney with dusty shoes and a mismatched suit. He became an attorney because his father was one and his grandfather was one. When Jesus was dragged into court, a member a Paul's family was probably a face in the courtroom.

Knowing the type of client he represents—mainly angry bitches seeking the death penalty for back child support—nine times out of ten he's the guy I'm battling in the mornings. If you need proof that we have no constitutional rights, then look no further than Orleans Parish Court. In this piece of shit judicial system, the judges have a financial incentive to find you guilty, and that's why most black men are found guilty. Even in child support cases, I had a client pay $11,500 to the court to avoid jail time, but the money was not received by that mother until nearly a year later. The judges used it however they saw fit until her attorney threatened to file suit. Those dirty bastards.

This is debtors' prison; this is a violation of the defendants' Fourteenth Amendment rights to due process and equal protection, but in the city of New Orleans, they don't give a teaspoon of a fuck about the constitution. Civil court is a business, the judges are franchise owners, and the defendants are the customers. You either pay up or go to jail—but not my clients, not today. My goal is to leave here paying the least amount or no additional increases and no fines. Fuck these judges, fuck Attorney Stein, and fuck these plaintiffs. Time to go to war

My first case this morning was a child support hearing that was continued pending the verification of my client's income. He's a writer like Jarvis at night, and a freelance journalist during the day. When he isn't writing, he spends the rest of his time shopping his manuscripts to publishers. He's hurting for cash. I took him on as a client as a favor to my mom; she is his godmother, so he's sort of like family. At our last hearing, I was found in contempt for blasting the judge after she publicly humiliated my client because of his weekly earnings and wanted him to find another job.

"Your Honor, with all due respect, have you considered finding another job? The audacity of the court to demean my client's legal livelihood is beneath this court and a grotesque abuse of your authority . . ." Yea, I was found in contempt.

The good news is I was successful in getting my client's case moved to another judge, and today, she granted the continuance for the verification. Any time my client leaves court without spending a dime, we consider that day a win.

My second client of the day's case was also continued pending the results of a paternity test. It wasn't my client who doubted whether he was the father—I did! That child didn't resemble either one of them. To add more methane to an already volatile situation, his new wife accompanied him to court today, because that's what they do. After court, new wife pulled me to the side to thank me for suggesting the paternity test. She'd had her own doubts, but didn't want to come off as the new wife who hated the existing kids.

"That bitch in court trying to pull off a heist—she knows that child is for her other baby daddy!"

"Well, there are two things you can always count on for the truth, and those things are saliva and blood. We will know the truth and the truth shall set him free." We shared a chuckle and afterward, I headed to the parking lot.

And wouldn't you know it—parked next to me was Attorney Stein.

"Ned, you've requested a *got-damn* paternity test after we've gone back and forth with this suit for almost a year?"

"Paul, you've seen my client and you've seen that kid— there's a better chance of you being the father than my client."

He hung his suit jacket on a hanger in the passenger seat of his Volvo XC90, then shot me a look from across the sunroof. Under his eyes were tea bags, and I could tell from the pot holes in his face that he's been hitting the bars a little too hard after work.

"Ned, you can't base it off the way the child looks. That's never a good indication."

"Burnt orange hair and green eyes? Paul, my client looks like LeBron James and the baby mama is from Wakanda."

"Ned, that's bullshit and you know it."

"Call it whatever you want, but I have already prepared a motion to dismiss plus a little something-something for the child support he's already paid—plus my fees."

Attorney Stein slammed his car door and floored it out of the parking lot.

Feeling good about my little victories in court, I wrapped it just in time for my lunch date with the love of my life.

After a short drive to mid-city, I arrived just in time for my lunch date with Yolanda. That's Attorney Yolanda Horne, if I must formally introduce. The meeting place was Neil's Restaurant, where the parking is a nightmare but the food is seasoned in the kitchen by Jesus.

There she was, seated on the patio in a tailored, fitted jacket and a tight, black skirt that looked mini—but she was sitting. From under the black skirt, those legs ran long as a river; covered in chic black hosiery, with majestic peaks and valleys, tightly crossed with one on top of the other. That's what made me step to her three years ago: those thick legs. I watched her for a second as if I didn't know her, as if I had just encountered her for the first time, and asked myself a life-changing question for which there was only one answer.

Would I still ask her out?

As beautiful as she is, as sexy as she is, as independent and accomplished . . . and even though she's the bad bitch I always wanted, the answer is no. I would not ask her out now.

Because I'm not on her level—not even close.

I come away from each interaction with Yolanda feeling inadequate, insufficient, and insecure. None of the aforementioned is her fault. The one thing a Ford and a Ferrari have in common is neutral, and neither will move in neutral unless pushed or pulled. Somewhere over the rainbow I shifted out of drive and came to a rolling stop in neutral. Everyone I graduated with has passed me by. I don't listen to the radio or watch TV because the commercials for their law firms torment me. Yolanda's career is hauling ass in the fast lane at 110 miles per hour, while I'm on the service road sitting at a red light.

The NOPD Union just hired Yolanda as their lead attorney, while my top client is Rasta, as you already know.

Yolanda was on a business call, so I glided in behind her chair and kissed her on the cheek. She softly caressed the side of my face. She'd already taken the liberty of ordering a lemonade for me, and chances are, she's already ordered my lunch: the shrimp fettuccine with a side of catfish, no salad, extra Cajun biscuit.

There was another couple just to the right of us: an older white gentlemen in a sports blazer with a younger African American woman of the same caliber as Yolanda. I struggled to hear their conversation, but whatever was said, the older gentleman found it hilarious.

Maybe a business lunch? Perhaps he's her regional supervisor?

The patio is on the side of the restaurant, which I remember used to be a huge single-family home with a side yard that's now the covered patio.

"Not a problem, Mr. Mayor, it's always a pleasure to work with you in Baton Rouge, and I look forward to a long and productive partnership as usual. I will see you in the morning."

She's doing big things, I gathered.

As she hung up the call, Yolanda's face instantly transformed from serious *business chic* to simply *my girl*.

She left her seat and made her way over to me. "Hi baby, I'm sorry about that." She leaned down and kissed me.

"That's never a problem; I always enjoy watching my baby

wheel and deal," I lied.

Every time I ear-hustle on one of her conversations, I come away feeling like a eunuch. Now I know why my uncle advised me against marrying a woman who makes more money than I do—over time you feel less like her husband and more like her pocket vibrator. At some point, she's going to want the latest model.

"How did it go this morning at civil court? It was two child support cases if I remember correctly?"

Yep, two measly little child support cases, as compared to your big-dog deal. "It went well; Judge Breaux was in a great mood, so I was able to knock both of them out before lunch."

"So Gail was nice to you this morning?"

Who she refers to as 'Gail' is none other than the Honorable Judge Gail Breaux, but to Yolanda, it's just 'Gail.'

"Now that I think about it, she was! Smiled at me and everything. Allowed my motion without an hour of back and forth. *I got to say it was a good day*," I declared in my Ice Cube voice.

"That's wonderful; I had lunch with her yesterday. Her husband is head of the police union." Her palm reached across the table. My palm instinctively slapped hers—my silly ass just high-fived my own emasculation. I'm nut-less!

"Oh, you had a conversation with her?"

"Well . . . I hope you don't mind; I just wanted her to know you were my little *booboo-skiiii*, that's all. Being that you have so many cases over there, I figured the mutual contact would make life easier for you."

Got-dammit! I didn't ask her to put in a word for me. That's the problem with her—she doesn't respect boundaries.

I smiled. "Good looking out for your little *booboo-skiii*." *Sidity bitch.*

The waiter appeared out of thin air with a tray of food balanced on the one hand and a serving caddy in the other. With great agility, he snapped open the caddy in a single motion, then placed the tray on top while another server refilled our drinks.

"Greetings, sir, I have our signature shrimp fettuccine with a sizzling side of catfish, no salad, extra Cajun biscuit." Yolanda had done it again.

Halfway through the meal, she wanted my undivided attention. "Telly, may I ask you a question?"

"Fire away."

"What are we doing?"

"Huh?" I played dumb, but I knew where this was going. "I'm having lunch with a beautiful woman on a gorgeous afternoon."

Her hair whipped in the breeze; there was zero humidity. My attempt to distract her with a synthetic compliment had failed. Yolanda is a Harvard-trained attorney.

She side-stepped my compliment with a blush, then reloaded her question. "Regarding *Telly and Yolanda,* what are we doing?"

"We love each other?"

"With the end goal being . . . what?"

"The end goal?"

"Telly . . ." Her left eye rose higher than the right.

"These last two to three years have been—"

"Thirty-eight months."

"The last three years have been amazing—"

"But?"

"Why do you feel there's a *but*?"

She flashed her bare Beyoncé hand. I hate that fucking song.

"I just need to know what we're doing here." The chewing stopped, the fork was set free, her arms folded. "I'm beginning to feel like dating is all you want—and I made it clear thirty-eight months ago what I wanted. I'm not getting any younger, and you have test-driven me enough. So, what are we doing?"

I was about to answer, but guess who entered the patio area with a woman who wasn't his wife?

"Yolanda, hold that thought one second—a good buddy of mine is seated behind you. I just want to say hi." I just wanted to dodge that question and be nosey. I walked over to his table.

"Don't I owe them Saints a beatdown?"

Jarvis nearly shit in his pants. "Mannn, what are you doing in my favorite restaurant?"

"Your restaurant? Dude . . . I told you about Neil's."

"Telly, this is Briana. Bri, this is Telly."

So that's Bri-Bri! Damn, she's sexy! Damn, she looks young!

"Nice to meet you, Briana," Yolanda stood.

I continued the introductions. "Yolanda, you met Jarvis at the Christmas party, and this is Briana." The group shook hands. I could tell Yolanda was taken aback by Briana. "Well, I will get out of your way and let you two enjoy your meal. See you tonight?"

"Yes sir, and you better have those Atlanta Falcons ready—last week they got plucked," Jarvis replied

"But not tonight!"

"We shall see."

"It was nice to finally meet you, Briana," I called as Yolanda and I returned to our table.

As soon as we turned, Yolanda whispered, "I thought his wife was . . ."

"I'll tell you about it later," I lied.

Once Yolanda was comfortably in her seat, I prayed she had lost her train of thought.

"As I was saying . . ."

Fuck, she remembered.

"I love you, and I love us. We could be the power couple in this city and dominate, but I can't make you want what I want." As soon as she finished that sentence, her phone alerted her to a call. "I'm sorry baby, but I have to take this. It's the chief."

I sat quietly for a few minutes, then noticed that she was packing up to leave. From what I could overhear, the call was regarding an officer-involved shooting that had taken place about an hour ago.

"Telly, I have to go. Let's finish this when you come over later," she whispered once she hung up her call. Then she gave me a cheeky kiss, like the kind you get in church, and disappeared like Wonder Woman.

Shortly after that, the waiter brought the check.

What the fuck did she order? The check came to ninety dollars plus tip. Then I spotted the two martinis. *This why I can't make a come-up.*

Yolanda doesn't know this, but I have two checking accounts. One of them is personal, and the other is commercial. Currently, the commercial is overdrawn by $640, and I have $1,700 in the personal. Chase Bank will automatically deduct one from the other because the accounts are linked. If you do the math, that leaves me with $1,140 minus the $90 lunch. I also have two pounds of weed from Rasta, but none of it is for sale.

I can't afford Yolanda, but that too is my fault.

We both have the same degrees and passed the same Bar exam, but she is making shit, bang, and pop while I'm six feet from broke. Yolanda just assumes I'm financially stable. That's the real reason I have avoided her marriage question for so long—I'm broke! The only reason I have the money you see in my personal account is because I met with Timothy on Monday, and he paid the cost of the divorce in full—pending court date in forty-five days!

That Tootsie girl better be worth it—that's all the advice I can muster up. Quitting his wife because she went from a size ten to a size eighteen is the dumbest reason in the world to leave a good woman, and to add to his stupidity, he has yet to try out the pussy. *Who does that?* That's why I'm not doing the marriage thing—I've watched too many people fall in love first and ask questions later. But hey, I'm in the divorce business, and idiots like Timothy are good for business.

After this ninety-dollar lunch, the only question I'm faced with is: Do I break up with Yolanda before the *Madden* tournament tonight, or after?

CHAPTER 12

1:30 p.m.

TELLY

A ninety-dollar meal and she didn't even request a to-go plate . . . but I did. For three years she has been a strain on my pockets, but it's not her fault. I was the one who gave her the impression that I was a baller. The worst part about lying to get a girl is when the lie actually works but you don't have the pockets to finance the lie. So I don't blame Yolanda, it's not her fault—she's just under the impression that her man has top-tier clients and the child support cases are favors for friends. The truth is, without the child support clients, I would be homeless.

It took me three years to admit it, but in hooking up with Yolanda, I bit off more than I can chew. So now I'm "Under Pressure" like David Bowie. If I could just get enough money for a few commercials, then I could get some real clients, like offshore rig accidents and mesothelioma—whatever the fuck that is.

From where I'm seated, Bri-Bri is facing me, and she hasn't blinked the entire time, looking at my boy with those *I'll fuck you on this table eyes*. It's starting to make sense now. The waiter returned with my receipt and bag that contained Yolanda's portion of the meal. Before I left Neil's Restaurant, I sent Jarvis a text:

Make sure to get that cheerleader from Bring It On home before eight o'clock.

I waved at Bri-Bri again on the way out. When I looked over my shoulder, Jarvis flicked me a *fuck you* from across the street. No sooner did I make it to my car than I received a call.

"Hey, sexy man!"

"Well hello to you too . . . I wasn't expecting this call."

"I had a gap in my schedule and wanted to see if you were somewhere near me?"

"Oh really? I love gaps. I'm five minutes away."

"Do hurry." The call ended.

Four minutes later, I entered the front door to find her seated at her kitchen table sipping a glass of white wine. I recognized the T-shirt she wore as one of my own, and from the side view of her thigh, I could tell she was naked under my black Nirvana shirt.

"Wow, you were really close."

"I just ran about four red lights, that's all. Hit a dude on a bike, side-swiped a mail truck, fucked up your flower bed out front . . . Cops are probably looking for me, but other than that, the drive over was a breeze."

"Well since you went through all of that trouble for me, guess I have to turn it up a notch for you."

"Let's make the most of this gap." I cuffed her by the pussy. She purred.

Meet Erica Wimberley!

I stumbled on her about a year ago at family court. I was running late that day and raced by her on my way into the court-room. She was seated on a bench out in the hall—crying. You don't know this about me, but I am a sucker for a damsel in distress—a woman on the side of the road with a flat tire, a surrogate father needed for a field trip, or in the case of Erica, a custody battle she was about to lose because she couldn't afford a lawyer.

Erica was a divorced mother of two little girls with an asshole ex-husband who wouldn't quit. He dragged her to court so much she lost her job at the auto auction, where she had been a title clerk. Now she works for Uber and collects about $620 a month from her ex-husband in child support. That's why he's still fighting her for custody—over $620 when Rasta has $950 for the same number of kids, but I digress. When I saw her on the bench crying, the judge had just given her a three-week continuance to hire an attorney. I lifted up her chin and represented her for free.

That led to this, and this is fucking amazing.

Erica is frugal; she rather watch Netflix than go to the movies. An outing with her girls consists of peanut butter and jelly sandwiches and bubbles in the park. I mainly see her during the day because she has zero time at night, and I am not ready to meet her daughters. They're ages seven and five, and pre-packed with forty-nine questions. My time with Erica is in between her Uber gigs and carpooling. That's what we call the Gap.

On one of the kitchen chairs, she straddled me.

Erica resembles Tracee Ellis Ross but has burnt orange hair and matching freckles. She is paper-thin; right on the line of malnourished but not quite. For over a year I have tried to put a little meat on her, but I think what happened is that during her struggle period, she would feed her kids and go to bed hungry. I know it's a fucked-up thing to say, but I keep Erica because I'm her Superman. Imagine that? With my broke-ass self, I found someone who had less, and it felt good. I didn't have to lie or front like I had more, nor did I have to remember any of the lies

I told, because my relationship with Erica started from a very honest place.

Deeply she kissed me, then stared into my soul. "Telly I'm ready."

"I can tell." I felt the heat and moisture on my crotch.

"No . . . I mean, I'm ready."

"Erica, I know you are, but you're sitting on it."

"No, silly. I'm ready for us to be a family. I'm ready for you to meet the girls. They're ready to meet you—the man who makes Mommy smile. I'm ready to wake up to you and feel what it's like when you come through the door in the evening. I'm ready to belong to you."

"So, in other words, you're saying you're . . . ready?" I said in my doofus voice; she started to pound on my chest. I stood straight up with her legs twisted behind my back. With both hands, she held my face and kissed me.

"Telly, I'm ready . . . you don't have live alone . . . move here with us."

"If you're sure?

"No man has ever protected me the way you do. Whether you marry me or not you are my angel."

Her words always build me up; Erica is the vitamin E to my ego. She appreciates everything I do. She writes me love letters. She sings to me in voicemails. She loves me!

"Erica . . . I'm ready."

Suddenly my phone rang. I switched Erica to my hip like my grandmother used to carry my sister around the house. By the time I made it to the table, I had missed the call.

"Take me . . . right there." Erica pointed behind me to the kitchen counter. I cleared a space between the sink, a coffer machine, a loaf of bread, and a Lysol container. She unbuttoned my belt and unfastened my slacks. My belt buckled clinked on the wooden floor. Erica did the rest. She took me inside, slow and steady.

In my right hand, I held a text from Yolanda.

Good news, baby! I added you as additional council for the police union; the contract is $210k annually, are you in?

Erica moaned in my ear, "Will you move in, and sleep with me every night?"

I replied to Yolanda and Erica with a single word.

"Yes!"

CHAPTER 13

Madden Night
6:20 p.m.

Tonight we are all here, but I haven't shared the news about the settlement. Diana and I decided to keep it a secret for as long as we can. Surprisingly, Diana still clocked in for her shift, but will put in her two weeks' notice. I asked her why two weeks? She said her grandmother told her to always give a job a notice whenever possible.

Don't take bad spirits to a new place.

Who could argue with the wisdom of a grandma?

On some Madden Nights like tonight, I much prefer to watch their interactions than play. I study them, and when my turn comes up, I pretend like something is going wrong in the kitchen. Once they substitute my name, I resume my case study and decipher the hidden messages in their expressions. How does the body remain with one woman while the mind is making love to another fifty miles away?

How can five guys be polar opposites and carbon copies all at the same time? There is one common thread I have found, and it's that none of them originated from homes where they witnessed a happily ever after. For instance:

Rasta: Father deceased.

Jarvis: Raised by grandmother.

Telly: Two-parent home but emasculated father.

Tim: Raised by single parent.

Biyell: Raised by single parent.

And I'm not making excuses for any of the guys in my living room, but when you have no point of reference, you sort of stumble through life until you figure it out. Theo had Dr. Huxtable, even JJ had James Evans, but some of these guys only had a momma, and therein lies the problem, in my opinion. In a woman, they either want someone like their mom or the total opposite. In either case, it's not fair. I think this is the reason I find the guys to be hypersensitive about some things and dangerously nonchalant about others.

If I attack the Rastafarian movement right now, it will spark an immediate reaction from Rasta. I can also trigger the reaction by simply calling him by his birth name, Roderick Ross. He's named after his father, and that name still hurts him. When his father died, they plopped him on the first pew in front of a coffin at seven years old. From that pew, he stared at a man who used to kiss him across his entire face. When that man died, that father-son affection was gone, and he learned to cope as best he could. Broken branches continue to grow and long as they're still connected to the root; abnormal growth is still growth.

One such branch is Roderick Ross, Jr., who grew up to become Rasta, a man with a giant hole in his chest and a debilitating fear of loss; a fear of having only one thing. Rasta went through life never trusting one person, and is still searching for answers in religion while stuffing as many women as he can fit into his chest cavity—the one left vacant by his daddy.

How could any woman fill that void?

How unfair is that to ask?

Not to pick on Rasta, but he should be banned from dating,

because no one has the answers to why his daddy died of cancer when he was seven. Furthermore, none of the women he's dated and destroyed ever bothered during courtship to ask that one simple question: *What is the most painful injury you've ever sustained?* I know that sounds too simple to reveal anything of value, but that's all his ex-wife, or LaDeisha or Shameka, had to do—ask him that simple question.

Allow me to demonstrate by using Timothy; he's seated on the loveseat, watching a game between Telly and Rasta.

The song blaring out of the speakers is "I Miss My Dawgs" by Lil Wayne, but I noticed that Timothy isn't smoking. He's spaced out again, laughing at jokes he didn't hear, and avoiding eye contact by any means necessary. I yelled over the top of Lil Wayne, and through the cloud, he found his way to the elevated portion of my kitchen counter.

"Telly tells me you're really going through with this divorce."

He looked over his shoulder at his empty seat at the edge of the sofa. "I'm done with this marriage, Uncle Glenn."

"So, what happens when Tootsie puts on a few extra pounds?"

"Uncle Glenn . . . it's not even about Tootsie—"

"That's not what I asked you."

Behind us, the guys just erupted in celebration because Crowd Noise Telly had talked a ton of shit the entire game and just blew a twenty-eight-point lead.

"What's going to happen when she goes from a size six to sixteen? Will you bust a move out the back door? Will you take the trash out one night like my cousin Pootie and then disappear into the fog? At what point are you in it for the long haul?"

"There you go sounding like Biyell." Like a tinted window, his agitation tried to block me from seeing the truth. "Why can't I like what I like? Why can't live this half of my life with the type of woman I find attractive? Why does that make me a horrible person?"

As Timothy cradled his phone, I noticed he was on Facebook.

"Is that your little sister Racee? The one who just graduated from Dillard?"

"Yes, that's her. That's my other sister Javonda, and that's my mom."

It was one of those graduation photos taken outside the commencement on a bright sunny day. At a quick glance, I could see that Tim shared the same body type as his sisters and mom. It didn't take a trained therapist to conclude that whatever was bothering him about Kayla's weight could have taken root as he was growing up.

"Do you have a current picture of Kayla?"

After a few seconds of scrolling, he landed on her profile page and clicked on a photo taken three weeks ago. It was a picture of her and several of her friends in a group shot. I could tell she was self-conscious about her weight; she only wanted the photographer to capture her from the side and posed to conceal her mid-section. She leaned forward like her back was in pain. I could also tell Timothy's rejection had taken a huge toll. In the photo, a very sad woman cried out for help; for shelter from his words, for a cool shade from his disdain, for some nook or cranny to hide from his disgust.

"Have you served her with the divorce papers yet?"

"No, Telly just handed me the papers today."

"Does she know?"

"No."

"So there's still time to reconsider."

"I'm unhappy." His face pruned.

Timothy couldn't hide his resentment. In the few minutes he was forced to view Kayla's Facebook page, I got a sense that it was unbearable for him. I have never seen a man fall so out of love so quickly. Maybe it was never love from the beginning?

"Have you told her you're ending this marriage, and that it's over as soon as she signs?"

Timothy clicked away from Kayla's profile and took his animosity out on his phone by powering it off completely. "She will know soon enough."

"Timothy, what's really going on?"

"Uncle Glenn, I told you, and it's not that complicated."

"That's what your mouth says, and that's what you want me to think. What's going on with you, Timothy?"

"I don't know what else to say. What else are you looking for?"

"Here's what I'm looking for . . . what was your breaking point with Kayla? Was it the photo shoot with that sexy Tootsie Roll?"

Annoyed, he said, "Uncle Glenn, just leave Tootsie out of it . . ."

"Let me see a picture of Tootsie."

"Leave. Tootsie. Out. Of. This! It's Kayla's big ass!"

Now I'm getting somewhere! My dad loved to say: *Whole truth is said during intoxication, anger, and a joke.* Timothy had just parked on the corner of Nigga Please and Fuck You Avenue.

"It's Kayla, it's her, she did this to us—she destroyed this marriage. I was happy, so don't blame this shit on me, Uncle Glenn. I was happy!"

"Timothy, I hear all that *Young and the Restless* shit you're talking, but when did you decide to walk away from her? When?!" I yelled.

"Last week!"

"Last week, Timothy?! Just last week? You paid $1,300 for a divorce based on a decision that was made last Thursday? Timothy, just think about this . . ."

Suddenly, the rage left his voice. "It was under the cabinet, in the bathroom. Who does that? In the bathroom . . ." His face became dark like a flat-screen. He eyes focused on the two cabinet doors right below my kitchen sink.

"Tim, what was under the cabinet in the bathroom?"

I'm not sure when it happened, but Jarvis's nosey ass managed to turn the music off, and the game had been paused.

"Last week, I-I reached under the cabinet in the bathroom looking for my hair clippers, and that's when I saw it."

"Saw what?" Jarvis asked.

"Shhhhhhhhh the fuck up," Telly said to Jarvis.

"Blue Bell ice cream."

"Under the bathroom sink?" Jarvis couldn't process it.

"JARVIS!" The room yelled.

"So she was hiding her food?" I encouraged Timothy to continue.

"It was all under there—empty cookie packages, empty ice cream tubs, Little Debbie snack cakes . . . It was all there. And every cookie, every cooking-spoon full of ice cream found a new home on her hips." With a tight fist, he repeatedly pounded my marble counter, but Timothy wasn't in my kitchen at that moment. He was under that bathroom sink. "I collected it all and confronted her."

"Have you ever considered that she snacked in the bathroom because you make her feel uncomfortable?" I asked.

"And that's what she said, but I wasn't aware I was doing it. The last time we were out to eat, she felt like I counted every spoon she put in her mouth. Like I measure the amount of time it took her to swallow. She said I frowned the entire dinner."

"Which only made her more depressed, and hide more food?"

"Yes, then she got angry and asked why she should lose weight for me. Why should I be the only one happy? I realized then that we are better apart than together. I no longer want to be the source of her unhappiness. We both deserve to be happy. And that's why I paid Telly."

"I understand, but I have one more question, then I will let it go. I promise."

With a nod, Tim permitted one more question—and only one.

"I remember you mentioned a while back that your parents divorced and never reconciled. Did you ever get the chance to ask your dad why he never tried to repair the marriage?"

A sigh came from the deepest part of Timothy's soul. "It was her."

"Another woman?" I asked.

"No, it was her. My mom. He said he couldn't take her anymore." Tim reached for a bar stool and took a seat for the first time since he walked over. "My mom has this thing when she gets angry. She talked to him real hard, and my dad wasn't the fussing type; he was the leaving type. Following him through the house, she would call him all kinds of *bitches,* telling him how he wasn't shit, and how she didn't need the *lil $350* he was contributing every week. She threw the money at him like my dad was a stripper. I watched my father collect his check off the floor. Then, he handed it to me, kissed my sisters, and asked me to get him a Glad bag from under the sink. He put his work clothes in the bag, and that was it. That was the last time he ever stepped foot in our house. My mom never apologized for castrating him in front of us, but shortly after that painful night . . . they divorced, and he remarried."

"How did things work out?"

"For my dad? I've never seen him happier. His wife—we call her Ms. Bunny—is the total opposite of my mom. My mom gave my dad hell dragging him back to child support court for increases, but he smiled through it all—which only made her more bitter."

"And how did things go for your mom?"

"I think she died the night he left, but rigor mortis never set in. She's bitter, bigger, and more bitchy."

The room fell silent for about two minutes, then there was a knock on the door. Everyone in the room looked at Biyell.

"What the fuck y'all looking at me for? I iced that bullshit about the dick picture last week!" Biyell assured us.

"How did you lie your way out of that?" I asked.

"I didn't have to. Three weeks earlier, we switched cell phone carriers, and Sprint data history was limited to the time WE ENROLLED!" Biyell screamed with joy.

"Lucky ass!" Telly called as he made his way down the hall to answer the door.

"So, who did you send the dick pick to . . . GiGi?" I asked.

"Nope, Mrs. Brown."

We all looked confused. "Mrs. Brown?"

"BOY, NO!" Rasta finally screamed. "The elderly lady with the milk and cake? The grandma you fucked?"

"Not fucked as in once upon a time, fuckinnnnggg as in lunchtime today!" Biyell confirmed.

CHAPTER 14

Madden Night
7:30 p.m.

W e were expecting company, and he arrived on time. It's strange, in this little group we have, how we often fight amongst ourselves, and how quickly we gang up against strangers. To our delight, Yonnis, the UPS guy, was accompanied by his brother, who carried his game controller in a miniature briefcase. The two new arrivals were greeted with everything from warm hugs to oven-baked ribs before Telly yelled out, "LOCK THE FRONT DOOR!"

Crowd Noise versus Yonnis!

Fight!

It didn't take Telly long—he got into their heads. Yonnis's favorite team was the Cowboys, but Telly marched his Falcons down the field with ease. Then came the noise.

"What! What! YOU CAME HERE TO SELL ASS? Ass on sale? HOW MUCH?"

"Two ninety-nine a pound!" Rasta yelled.

"That's too damn high for cheap ass!"

"Two-fifty!" Biyell yelled.

"HELL NO!"

Then we all yelled, "ASS ON SALE, TWO-TEN A POUND!"

Yonnis just smirked and nodded, but he didn't have an answer for Crowd Noise. His Cowboys fumbled on the goal line right as they were about to score. The Falcons recovered the fumble and ran it back ninety-ninety yards the other way. Crowd Noise cranked the volume up to ten!

"HOT BUTTERMILK ASS ON SALE! WALMART CAN'T MATCH TWO-TEN A POUND!

Telly beat Yonnis 21–0, but I think he intimidated the young man with his taunting routine. That was the consequence *selling ass cheap*. Next up was Yonnis's brother Michael versus Jarvis.

I waved for Telly to join me at the kitchen counter: my preferred place watch the weekly tournaments. The stools make it easier on my good leg. If you're wondering why I don't use my prosthetic, the answer is simple: I never adjusted to it. I never gave the damn thing a chance. I never made it through that bruising and swelling period, and to add to it, Diana, who turns counter-clockwise throughout the night, kicks my bad leg during each rotation.

Did I mention how much I hate my wheelchair?

I'd rather centipede across the floor.

But enough about me and my leg. Telly eased onto the stool recently vacated by Timothy.

"You sent me a text earlier around lunchtime that said remind you to tell me about Jarvis. What about Jarvis?" I asked

"That's right, I almost forgot. I had lunch today at Neil's— that new spot in Mid-City—when in comes . . ." Telly pointed a discreet finger over at Jarvis, "and *soul-sucker Bri-Bri*."

"Get the fuck out of here! At lunch? Middle of the day? On a work day?"

"Uncle Glenn, she looks really young."

"How young?"

"Like, *To Catch A Predator* young. Like nigga, you better

check her ID young."

"But he said she's twenty-six . . . if I remember correctly?"

"That may be true, but she looks every bit of seventeen to me."

"Whoa, that young, huh?"

"I know he said the sex was fire, but I like grown women, who look grown. The only thing Bri-Bri can do for me . . . is introduce me to her momma."

"I pleaded with Jarvis to cut her loose a few weeks ago—that night was supposed to be the last time," I said.

"The last time? Jarvis is hooked like a crackhead!"

"Did you say that restaurant was in Mid-City?"

"Right off Canal Street."

"His wife works at the Cox Cable building on Canal—a few blocks away. It sounds to me like Bri-Bri has sucked all the common sense out of Jarvis."

"Done sucked him stupid."

"I'll have a chat with him for sure. By the way, how are things going with you and Dos?" The code name for Yolanda is Ms. Dos, because she is *two-fine*!

"I don't know; it's hard when your lady makes more money than you and expects you to maintain on her level, but for what it's worth, she did throw me a bone earlier, a contract doing some legal work for the police union. At first, I told her yes, but as I thought about it—I should back away from it."

"Why? If you two are working toward a future together, then why does it matter who makes the most money, and why turn down a contract?"

"Like Timothy, my mom also made more money than my dad, and he hated her for it. He would always say, *Never let a woman buy your shoes*."

"Huh? Why not?" I was confused on this one.

"Because when *mad day* comes, she will tell everyone, *I bought everything on his body, from his hat to the shoes on his feet*. Never let a woman buy your shoes."

"I hear you, Captain Caveman, but if you had the right woman, then you wouldn't have that to worry about."

"Uncle Glenn, we're not all blessed like you with a Lady Diana. You guys have a storybook life. Hell, you're the only happily married couple I know."

"Oh, so you were under the impression things have always been like this?"

"Seems that way, and since you're always asking us questions, how about I ask you one?"

"Fire away."

"Let's say you never had that accident at work—would you and Diana still have this marriage?"

"So, your premise is our marriage is happily ever after because I need her?"

"I didn't mean any offense," Telly said in an apologetic tone.

"None taken . . ."

"I'm just wondering because I'm in the divorce business."

"Emphatically, yes! I would still be with Diana. By the time that junkie backed over me with that forklift, Diana and I were already twenty years locked. The work I put in now is the same work I put in on week one. In our case, things started bad; then we were forced to separate the bullshit from the soil. That's how we built our marriage: on a solid foundation of communication. And here is God's honest truth: I never thought about leaving my wife even when I had two good legs."

From across the room, I saw Rasta stand up straight as a light pole with every cell in his brain focused on his phone. *Here we go again*. This is how it always starts; the guy is having a good time with his buddies, then he receives a text or a call—normally it's a text. Judging from the seriousness in his face, this text could only be from one of two people. LaDeisha or Shameka! Rasta just managed to patch things up with Shameka, so my guess is he has just read something from LaDeisha.

Like Jarvis, like Biyell, like Timothy, like Telly, Rasta is also torn between the woman he needs and the woman he wants. Each woman is playing a unique role in his life, one that is equally important. From across the room, I watched Rasta dap off the crew as he moved in my direction. It's not like Rasta to leave this early; something is wrong.

"Hey Unc, I need to cut out a little early tonight, but looks like y'all don't need my help with Yonnis and his brother."

"It looks that way. So, where you off to so early?"

"LaDeisha just hit me up, she needs me to come over. She says it's urgent."

"Everything all right, huh? You need the calvary?" Telly offered.

"I appreciate that, but it sounds like some Category One-type shit. Now, if you get a 911 text, then that means come get me because she stabbed me in the chest." Rasta laughed his way out the door and hurried to LaDeisha for his urgent meeting.

I hope he hasn't gotten that girl pregnant.

CHAPTER 15

9:05 p.m.

LADEISHA

It was fun in the beginning—finally having a man who wasn't obsessed with swimming up the political gutters of New Orleans. It was also wonderful to have a man who could create works of art from a piece of wood and his bare hands. I used to sit in his garage, which he converted into a wood-working studio, for hours watching him and never grew tired. Then I'd ride along with him like Take Your Girl to Work Day and watch him sell the same tribal mask for hundreds of dollars. Roderick's ability to generate a living from thin air made me respect him in a way I'd never respected any other man. Then life happened to me and changed my landscape.

If only I didn't have the mother I have—then I could enjoy the simpler things in life like a store selling our artwork, but the pressure she applies is unbearable. She's so accomplished, so respected, so perfect, and so aware of it. She forces us to be mindful of our contacts and relationships at all times. We represent her, as she always says.

"I am preparing the way for you so that your travel will not be troublesome," My mother said to me just this morning. That translates to, *Don't fuck it up.*

At this point in my life, I just want to enjoy being a thirty-six-year-old woman who is child-free but ready to be with child. I'm ready to be a wife. And if I never make it to Congress to replace my mother, then I'm happy being the president of the PTA. As long as my future husband loves me and our future kids are healthy, I consider that a successful life. These are words I would never utter in the presence of my mother, because the first thing she would want to know is, *Who is the future husband?*

She hates Roderick as much as a woman could hate her daughter's boyfriend. At one point she did attempt to be cordial, but her idea of cordial quickly flushed into cordially insulting. And my father isn't much better. He never looks Roderick in the eye; instead he looks at the hairnet that holds his dreadlocks as if it's the most hideous thing he's ever seen. The night he met my parents, I couldn't have been prouder of Roderick. He wore slacks and a blazer just for me, and he stood chest-to-chest with my father, despite how my family scowled at him the way white merchants once treated black customers who dared to sit at their lunch counters. Funny how this thing called classism isn't practiced exclusively by one particular race. Isn't it ironic—don't you think?

Tonight, I told Roderick to come over because my mother has once again micromanaged my life and placed the weight of all humanity on my shoulders. My doorbell just sounded; it's Roderick. His face looks filled with worry. I was short of details in my text, but I couldn't risk anything getting lost in translation. I needed to see him face-to-face.

I kissed him hello. He took a seat on the sofa while I grabbed a chair near the breakfast nook.

"Baby what's going on? I got here as quickly as I could."

"Before I get started, are you hungry?"

"No, I had plenty to eat at Uncle Glenn's."

"That's right, today is Thursday. Silly me forgot again."

"It's no problem, LaDeisha, what's going on?" His eyes widened with concern. Beads of sweat huddled on his forehead and temples. His dark chocolate skin was melting on the sides. His left leg pattered up and down like he was playing a drum set. If I don't tell him soon, he may catch a heart attack.

"Remember we discussed the possibility of me making a run for the Louisiana State Senate?"

"Yeah, I remember. I even offered my crew to help with the campaign."

"I don't know how to say this, but here it goes . . . I'm not running for the State Rep seat."

He appeared relieved. "But you put in so much grassroots work in preparation to run—what changed?"

"My mother. She's retiring; I'm going to run for her seat."

I watched his back give out as he sunk like a battleship into the sofa; it was as though he knew what I was about to say.

The air turned cold and stale. "At every red light on the way here, I said to myself, *We're having a baby.*"

"I wish."

"Why wish?" He backed me into a corner.

"Because, because . . ."

"Because LaDeisha Marie Barthelemy is about to run for Congress and it's time to off Rasta Man! *No, no, no,* can't have a weed-head in your midst. Isn't that what you mother said?"

"Roderick, I never felt that way about you, and you promised me after our last argument that you wouldn't take your anger out on me for the way my parents feel about our relationship."

"Then why did you have me rush over here?"

"To say I'm so sorry . . ."

"Sorry? For what? What are you so sorry about?"

I tried everything to hold back the tears, but his watery eyes created scattered clouds of sadness. "I didn't want things to end this way . . ."

"So it's over?"

"It has to be."

"Says who?" He rose with anger and hovered over me like a giant hot air balloon filled with flammable hurt. "The last time I checked, you're thirty-six years old. In the state of Louisiana that makes you a consenting woman, so please explain to me why our relationship has to end."

"Because you will never pass vetting!"

"But you vetted me three years ago . . . you approved me. What other qualifications must I pass to continue my job as your man?"

"None, Roderick, but politics is dirty, and they will dig into your past and—"

"And my nickel and dime arrests will cost you the election. So it's not your mother, it's you. You're phasing out my job title in your life. You're laying me off. It's you."

I reached for him, but he pulled away and walked to the farthest corner of the room. All I see are his endless shoulders and a back as wide as the Motherland. I want to run to him, but I can't. To hold him, but I'm not naive. To tell him how much I love him, but I know that means little right now.

"All day I tried to find the right words to say, but everything spoken tonight was the incorrect verbiage. I have enjoyed my time with you, and I couldn't have asked for a better man. The task before me is bigger than me; this congressional seat cannot fall into the wrong hands. It could be devastating should that happen."

Roderick removed his dread cap and slowly turned to face me. "What do you want me to do?"

"Roderick, don't make this more difficult than it already is . . ."

"Just name it, what? Anything?" He took long slow steps back to the breakfast nook. "You want me to cut my hair? Then get a pair of scissors; fuck it. You want me to stop smoking weed? Then come home with me and watch as I flush it all." He kneeled to one knee in front of me. "Do you want me to clean up my record? I will spend all I have to get my record expunged and sell all of my inventory and tools and give all the money to my ex. I'll put the money in her hand and beg her to drop the child support case."

He buried his head in my lap. His tears were warm and plentiful. On both sides of my legs, his dreadlocks draped to the floor and felt like a warm, wool blanket. I couldn't help but notice how perfectly we melanized together; seamlessly, like a swirl of dark pottery. Maybe in another life he was my king and I was his queen of a tribe in Ghana—or Chad, or even Angola—but it was not meant to be. Not for us.

"I have worked day and night trying to get my life in line. I knew this day was coming—I felt it—but give me just a little more time, LaDeisha. Tell me, what do you need me to do?"

I don't know what to say!

He would do all of that for me?

He would change everything? Give up everything?

He's willing to do anything to keep me; he's fighting for me.

No one has ever fought for me. I could be making the biggest mistake of my life in ending this relationship. Maybe I should take some time to think about it . . . but who am I kidding? There isn't anything to think about; those political PAC would have a feeding frenzy on Roderick. Every political ad would paint him as the biggest drug dealer in New Orleans, and it would kill my mother to hand her enemies an easy win, especially when it's my seat to lose.

"I'm sorry Roderick, but I have to get off this wonderful ride right here. This is my stop."

It was the trembling of his bottom lip that ripped my heart out of my chest. I never in life have caused a man that much pain. He offered me all he owned, and I could not accept it because of my duty; it's my commitment to this legacy I never valued. This life of politics devours the weak and frail. It can turn a monster into a president and a righteous man into a pariah in less than three hours. I love Roderick too much to subject his personal life and his kids to the wolves in Washington. It nearly destroyed my parents' marriage because it stripped my father of his rightful role as head of household—the only thing in life he cherished.

Whereas my father was prepared and equipped for the heat the comes with the spotlight, I know Roderick is not.

"Goodbye Roderick, thank you for the ride."

He rose this time like the sun hidden behind stubborn gray skies. Before he crossed the room to the door, he removed my door key from his key change and set it on the table. Then, with a light step, he exited my home. It was over. It was done. I felt like shit, but it was for the best, I guess.

The first step was complete, so I took the second. I reached for my cell phone and placed the call. When the voice answered, I said, "It's over and he's gone." Then, I ended the call. I gave my word and I kept my word. LaDeisha and Rasta are no more.

As I turned toward my bedroom, I felt something soft under my toes. When I looked down, there was a yellow, red, and green netted cap right where Roderick had left it—a little bit of him he wanted to me keep. I feel like shit.

I love you too, Rasta Man.

CHAPTER 16

Madden Thursday
March 23, 2017
1:10 p.m.

KAYLA

I took the tour, I like the vibe, and I said yes to the pitch . . . but most of all, I said yes to me. I am officially a member of a little gym filled with average, everyday people—somewhere I can blend in with the herd and work on myself. It's only nineteen dollars a month. In the worst-case scenario, I will come three times a week for the Aqua Massage—that alone is worth the cost of membership. But like I said, this is for me, and it feels good to look around this room and see other women like me. It's very comforting.

Directly in front of me is a floor-to-ceiling mirror that stretches the full length of the gym. Yes, a got-damn mirror. It's like I'm seeing myself for the first time. *Who are you and what did you do with Kayla?*

The trainer set my treadmill for one mile, as if that's a minor request. I haven't walked a mile in ten years, and I haven't jogged since college. I'm on a treadmill with a goal of finishing this mile in eighteen minutes. It wasn't so long ago I could run this mile in ten minutes and thirty seconds, but that's back when I was an athlete, raining down spikes of fire over the volleyball net.

When did I cease to be an athlete? How did I go from Xavier University Volleyball to this? Winded on a treadmill after only five minutes? Pitiful.

To the left of me is a little petite girl no more than twenty-one, zoned out with ear buds. Just look at her go! Running like she's being chased by inmates at Angola Prison. God, I miss those days when I could run like that, with that body. To the right of me is another lady about fifty years old. She's lapping me. *Stop it, Kayla.* You're not here to compete, you're here to spend productive time alone and reconnect with Kayla—that's it.

But who am I?

Did I really allow this to happen?

When did I take on the likeliness of my Aunt Joyce?

When I married him I thought I was safe and could relax in love. Because love is forever, right? Somewhere in this marriage, I lost Kayla and started caring more about what he wanted and needed. I lost myself.

"Kayla, you are 125 pounds overweight, and with your family history, I need you to get serious. I don't want the lip service, and I don't want to hear how depressed you are—you will not have anything to be depressed about in the grave. I had a patient a year younger than you, refused to follow my health plan for her life; heart disease killed her last night. She caught a heart attack in a restaurant while having dinner with her husband. Her last meal was everything I begged her to avoid. I'm not going to lose you! I need you to exercise three days a week. Are we clear?"

When he said those words to me, it didn't feel demoralizing and insulting. Even to my own amazement, I received his message. Then again, I've been a patient of Dr. Cleaves since high school. However, similar words spoken by my husband felt like the difference between summer and winter. That's why I'm here, and the woman in the mirror is here—but I don't know her.

In my mind, I am still Kayla Da Spike, with the abs and quads and zero fat ratios. Guys use to mistake me for Rhianna, and I was just as furious. In my mind, I am still the girl local rappers wanted in their videos. I modeled for Macy's and Bronner Bros. International Beauty Show in Atlanta, and at the Essence Music Festival.

That's how I met Timothy. I should've declined his dinner invitation after that photo shoot, but there was something different about him.

Damn! I just reached half a mile? This treadmill is broken—it has to be!

But anyway, back to what I was saying. Back then I didn't date fat guys, but he was cute, and he made me laugh. My God, I laughed for hours, and that's how he hooked me. On my checklist of must-haves, he only received three checks. I made concessions on seven essentials like:

- Never married
- No kids
- Athletically built
- Financially stable
- Two-parent home
- College degree, preferably advanced

And last but not least:

- Girth!

Quite a few concessions, to be sure, but I made an exception and allowed him into my heart on the Affirmative Action plan. For the first six years of this ten-year marriage, I basked in the rays of his affection. Then winter came. With each pound of fat I gained, the temperature dropped. The vacations ended, the early work days just to make love ended, the spontaneous gifts ended, and those random phone call throughout the day ended. We went from having sex four times a week minimum to four times a month—eventually it went to four times a year, and only after he watched porn all night.

One minute to go and I'm getting close to that mile.

I helped him keep his business above water; I maxed out my credit cards buying camera equipment and he hasn't snapped one picture of me. I even used my modeling contacts to get him freelance projects. I know I sound like the soundtrack from *Waiting to Exhale*, but I was that woman to him—even after our marriage became blistering cold, even after he warmed other women with the same rays of light that once baked my skin to bronze. I never changed, I never shifted. I did the impossible; I remained the same consistently loving woman to a man who didn't deserve it. Now I must be that woman to myself.

BEEP, BEEP, BEEP, BEEP!

Wouldn't you know it—one mile in sixteen minutes, four seconds! Here comes the trainer!

"You go, girl! I owe you an apology! There really is an athlete hidden inside of you. I am so proud of you, Kayla—we're going to have fun getting you active again."

Kelly's lips were moving, but I couldn't hear anything after *I'm so proud of you*. Those five little words were powerful enough to bring out the sunshine. Those five words healed something within me; I'm not sure what, exactly, but I do know I felt a little bit better than I did before I joined.

"Kayla, I'm so proud of you!"

She said it again, but this time I felt a jolt in a different part of my body. I grabbed my water bottle and towel, and she led me in the direction of the locker room. I needed to get there quickly; I couldn't hold it much longer. I zoomed through the maze entrance that led to the women's locker room and blew through the door of the first available stall. I made it just in time; the tears fell like marbles of painful hail. Kelly's face morphed into Timothy's face, and her healing words were replaced with lashes from his leather tongue. It was a hailstorm, and I was exposed.

Then came another ray of light.

A gentle voice susurrated in my soul:

It's me; I'm in here, I've been here the entire time. Do you remember me? Do you remember my dreams? The places I wanted to go? The life I wanted to live with someone who loved me? Do you remember Kayla? Her ambition? Your husband told you in a fit of rage that he didn't waive his right to a preference when he married you. I've been waiting to remind you that you didn't waive your right to happiness when you married him. If you remember me, then release me. I want out of here. I want to live again. I want to love myself again.

After a ten-minute drive, I pulled into my driveway and parked on the side of Timothy's car. I process my mortgages from home; his car is never here at this time. When I entered the kitchen door, he was standing in the corner by the pantry shuffling through the mail.

I looked down at him—not in conceited manner, but I'm six-foot-two and he's five-foot-eight wide and round. He wears two shirts at all times; a T-shirt and button-up that he never buttons up. His pants are always quarter-length shorts, but I call them capris for men, and he goes to three more hair appointments than I schedule for myself each month.

When I entered the room, he gave me this nervous look—not like the look I normally get. He looked at me like he was sizing me up, like were two heavyweight fighters before the bell. Maybe I should punch him in the face . . . but with my luck, I would be the one in jail. Timothy is not worth me getting arrested and losing my broker license while he moves another skinny bitch into my house. His hands are on his hips and he's staring up at the ceiling. On the table facedown is a stapled stack of legal paper, next to it a pen. Oh my God, that explains the check to Telly Ned for $1,390. *This is it.*

"Kayla, I didn't want it to come to this, but it has."

"Come to what?" I acted oblivious.

"We're too young to be this miserable."

"I'm sorry, but I don't recall a conversation where you asked me how I feel. So how did you conclude that I'm miserable?" *No, motherfucker, be a man and say it, but it's not going to go like you rehearsed.*

"Come on, Kayla . . ."

"Come on, my ass . . . how do you figure I'm miserable?"

"Look, the last thing I want to do right now is argue. I feel that—"

I cocked my head to one side. "I'm not arguing. I'm trying to figure out when you became an expert on my feelings."

"I don't want . . . this marriage anymore."

"Say what you really mean: you don't want me anymore."

Suddenly, I started to hear the voice that spoke to me in the gym; the voice that reminded me of who I am.

When he finally says it, you will not cry. Do you understand?

Yes.

He has caused you enough pain, but this time you're not going to run to the bathroom and cry. This final time, you will stand here like a big girl and not give him the benefit of seeing how much he has hurt you. Do you understand?

Yes, I will stand strong.

"Kayla, I don't want you." He sounded winded, like he barely had the strength to push the words out of his mouth.

There, he said it. That wasn't so bad. Now flip over those divorce papers and make him wait while you read every page.

When I reached for the papers on the table, it startled him because I guess he was anticipating a tornado of tears and snot—but my mother told me, *If a man has made you cry twice in the same day, you're with the wrong man.* I read through all eleven pages and counted seventeen typos—his lawyer isn't worth shit if I decided to fight this—but it was a basic, non-contested divorce. It was printed on the same divorce template I downloaded for free and added his name to, but never printed.

"My only condition for this divorce is I want the house sold because it's in my name. Whatever proceeds come from the sale I will split with you. Agreed?"

There was a delay in his response, but after a minute he agreed.

"I will email you the amendment to attach, but for now I will write it in on this copy."

After I specified my conditions in writing, the only sound in the room came from the hum of the refrigerator and that pen dragging across those divorce papers. I slid my copy to him and waited for his signature. For a brief moment I saw a twinkle of hurt in his eyes—or it could have been an out-of-place eyelash. But in any case, the voice was right; I denied him that one final slap, that one final hawk-spit, and left his ass with the last lick.

"I expect that you will vacate the house within two weeks; it's going up for sale in the morning."

After a hard swallow, he agreed.

I went to what used to be our bedroom and took a long, hot shower. Then did something I haven't done in a year: I decorated my face with pretty colors and found the skimpiest outfit in my closet. Then, I packed two suitcases and called my momma. I didn't have to explain; all I said was, *I'm coming home.*

"Kayla, your room is waiting for you. Come on, baby."

Before putting my car in reverse, I took a long look at the house that started as a home but became a prison. I blew it a soft kiss goodbye, then backed out of the driveway.

Good job, Kayla, I'm so proud of you.

Welcome back.

CHAPTER 17

Madden Night
6:20 p.m.

John Madden sat patiently waiting for the tournament to start, but he and the PlayStation controllers would have to wait a little while longer—something was off. Only three of them had arrived thus far, and one of those was Timothy. He wore a funeral expression on his face, which I found confusing. Kayla had given him everything he wanted, but his face was as long as a football field.

On Timothy's right was Jarvis, who still couldn't believe that Timothy went forward with the divorce, and on his left was Biyell, who was being a lot more compassionate than I expected.

Guess he figured why kick Timothy when he's down?

I know it may be difficult to feel sorry for a guy like Timothy. After all, he threw away a good woman for something as miniscule as weight, but in his mind, her weight was something that happened to him. I know that sounds crazy, but in the minds of men like Timothy, the weight gain issue is a sign of disrespect. For that reason, I applaud Kayla for making a quick exit. When some men feel disrespected, they disrespect twice as hard.

While I was busy contemplating Timothy's situation, Biyell received a phone call and stepped into the kitchen area near me to answer it. It was GiGi. There's that look of horror again. Biyell's hand raised to his forehead as if he had a fever.

"No, I didn't check my email yet," Biyell said into the phone. Then he started to pace from the sink to the counter and back like the ball on a laptop screensaver. On cue, Jarvis quit the pity party for Timothy and came into the kitchen. We all know Biyell's body language. Judging by the way he reacted to what GiGi just told him, we are experiencing what we refer to as a Cat-Five Crisis.

Biyell ended the call and bent over like an Olympic sprinter at the end of a hundred-meter race.

"Biyell, what's up man? Sounds like that call went south on you," Jarvis inquired.

"Don't tell me someone died," I worried.

"I died," Biyell replied.

"Hot Boy, what are you talking about?" Jarvis asked.

"That was GiGi!"

"Well, I figured that much. What's going on?"

"Dumb shit."

Biyell was broken over like Shaq had just kicked him in the nuts. Jarvis went and stood next to him and crouched near his ear.

"What's going on? Let's talk about it." Jarvis was consumed with curiosity.

Suddenly, Biyell's phone sounded again. He answered.

"Hey, Tyra."

Inaudible.

"I am excited; I rushed off the phone because it was my turn on the game."

Inaudible.

"The truck will not be an issue, but when are you due to report?"

Inaudible.

"You caught me off guard, that's all. I was with you yesterday and you never mentioned it. I want to do it right—let's push it out at least thirty days.

Inaudible.

"Because that's going to be hard to find, but let me get right back to you on that."

Inaudible.

"I love you too . . . nothing is wrong. The guys are waiting for me. We will talk more tonight." He ended the call.

Slowly, Biyell rose to an upright stance. Then, he looked up toward the heavens.

"Lord, if you get me out of this, I promise I am gonna live right!" Biyell prayed the prayer of the guilty.

"All right, lay it on us," I said.

"GiGi was just approved for a transfer to New Orleans. She says she's tired of the long-distance relationship."

"So that was the *thirty days* part of the conversation?" Jarvis asked.

"Yes, that's thirty days to find us an apartment."

"Bruh, hold up! GiGi doesn't know about Tamera?" Timothy asked.

"She never asked."

"Biyell! She never asked? Why didn't you tell her up front?"

"She never asked, I never volunteered. I figured she's in Baker, which is north of Baton Rouge, so there's zero chances of Tamera and GiGi crossing paths . . ."

"And what do I say all the time about getting busted?" I reminded him.

"It's not the things you can control that get you busted—it's the things out of your control," Jarvis recited.

"So, she's under the impression you're living with . . . ?"

"You." Biyell wasn't specific.

"Who?" I asked.

"You, I live with you, Uncle Glenn! It was the perfect lie. It worked—I'm here a lot."

"Wait! Wait, hold up a minute. She was down here for Christmas, but you didn't come here, so how did you pull that off?"

"My sister flies to San Diego on Christmas to be with her husband, who is retiring in a few months from the military. Being that I was house-sitting, we spent Christmas there."

"And Tamera? How . . . bruh? How did you pull that off?"

"Two days prior to Christmas, I would work on call to replace the money spent on Christmas—she never questioned it."

"Except you were with GiGi?" I confirmed.

"Yes."

And there you have it—a world wide web of lies, all connected to the others. I don't feel sorry for Biyell, and I don't appreciate him telling GiGi that he lives with me. That poor girl; she doesn't know Biyell has a nearly identical family here in New Orleans, and that his mistress is over six months pregnant. Now it's clear why he became stressed the fuck out. GiGi will be here in thirty days. Before I jump his shit about including me in his lies, I need to know if he plans to tell her the truth before she packs up and moves.

"So, when are you going to sit GiGi down and tell her the truth?" I asked. "Biyell, if you feel anything for her, then come clean."

"Mannn, fuck!" With both hands, he covered his eyes.

"Biyell, there comes a time when you have to take your lick. You have lied to her, you have included me in the lie—which I don't appreciate—and your wife doesn't know."

"But she will know—real soon. It's already done."

"Did Tamera find GiGi's phone number when she conducted that shakedown strip-down?" Jarvis wanted to know.

"No, that transfer request I told you about earlier . . . it's to Child Protective Services on the Westbank Expressway."

"Get the fuck out of here!" Timothy said as he headed for the door. "On that note, I need to take a walk."

"In the same building," Biyell continued. "Tamera was just

hired by Child Protective Services on the Westbank Expressway in the same building. GiGi works at the state level, which means . . ."

"*Your wife is now working for your mistress!*" I couldn't believe it.

I grabbed my crutch and followed Timothy outside. Jarvis followed me, leaving lying-ass Biyell in the kitchen alone. Even the crew couldn't stomach his bullshit this time.

CHAPTER 18

Madden Night
7:12 p.m.

Madden Night was off to a horrible start, and we needed some fresh air. We left Biyell alone inside and reconvened on the tailgate of Jarvis's truck. Though none of us had met GiGi, we had compassion for her. I planned to stay on Biyell until he fixed it. The part of that story he'd omitted—but I knew in full detail—was that GiGi's grandfather died recently and left her twelve rental properties all over Baton Rouge. And if that wasn't appealing enough, five of the properties were located three blocks from Tiger Stadium, and LSU had just raised their offer. GiGi was Biyell's ticket into a game he couldn't afford—the real estate game.

As Timothy, Jarvis, and I made ourselves comfortable around Jarvis's truck, Rasta's truck screeched into the driveway. Seconds later, Shameka's car screeched in after him. Judging by both of their twisted, sullen faces, something was definitely wrong.

Rasta hopped out of the truck and ran over to us.

"What's going on, Rasta Man?" I asked as I gestured toward Shameka, who was angrily climbing out of her car.

"Some bullshit," Rasta replied. "Hey Jarvis, can I load my shit in your truck and get a ride home tonight?" As he spoke, Rasta shot a death glance at Shameka.

Jarvis chucked his truck keys to Rasta. "Brother, take my truck and drive yourself. Take as long as you need."

Despite his constant conflict with women, Rasta is one of those guys that people will do anything for because of his generosity. For years, Rasta has supplied all of us with free weed; never asks for a dime and would never take a dime. When Jarvis build his new house, Rasta asked his wife to provide pictures of her dream cabinets—not the cabinetry in her budget, but her dream. Rasta crafted those dream cabinets for her, plus the crown molding to match. He refused to accept a payment.

"At least I know if I'm ever homeless, I have somewhere to take a bath and lay my head for a night or two," he always says. That's Roderick 'Rasta Man' Ross.

Even this custom-made crutch I use was carved out of a single piece of wood to my exact measurements—Rasta refused to accept a penny. When Biyell and Timothy had a fight in my living room and broke the coffee table, it was Rasta who worked through the night to build another one before Diana made it home.

With Shameka following and fussing, Rasta unpacked the truck. Only once all the items were removed did he address Shameka. Immediately, Jarvis hauled ass into the house and returned with his laptop to document every word.

"Have I ever called you a bitch?" Rasta demanded in a deep, thundering voice.

"This is how you handle me—" Shameka began.

"Have I ever called you a bitch?" his voice boomed.

"No, but that doesn't excuse the—"

He clipped her in mid-sentence. "Didn't I tell you last time if you ever disrespected me again by calling me a bitch, that was the end of us?"

"Roderick, this is fucked up what you're doing . . ."

"I'll tell you what's fucked up—dealing with a woman like you. Letting you get away with calling me *bitches* and *hoes* because I needed this truck. I'll catch the bus with my shit before I deal with you another minute. *You told me an hour ago in front of your friends that this is your truck and I can't do shit without you*—watch this." For the second time in a week, Rasta returned a key.

After securing all his belongings in the bed of Jarvis's truck, Rasta left Shameka standing there with both vehicles. And just like that, her control over him was broken. Rasta was free.

We returned to our usual seats in the living room—well, everyone except Jarvis. Like a grandmother on watch, he continued to peek out the window at Shameka. "She still out there; I wonder who's coming to help her move the truck?"

I couldn't care less; my attention had shifted back to Biyell. Rasta's life was instantly simplified—in part by his own doing, and in part by LaDeisha's, but he was free. Rasta had filled me in on the details of his breakup with LaDeisha as soon as it happened. The way I see it, LaDeisha made an executive decision based on what was best for her life. That decision did not include Rasta, but at least she was brave enough to make that decision.

On my loveseat sat a man who would soon have two women on the same track, heading at each other at eighty miles per hour. He holds the lever. Only Biyell has the power to prevent another derailment. Men like Biyell continue to cause derailments because of their inability to commit to a single track—to one woman. He has never liquidated a relationship with integrity and respect before entering into another romantic partnership. Come to think of it, none of these guys—not Biyell, nor Jarvis, nor Timothy, nor Telly, nor Rasta—ever handle any of these women with a thread of decency.

And it has gotten out of control.

Spiraling.

Snaking.

Sinking.

All because of their inability to pull the lever. To switch the tracks. To make a decision.

"Biyell, what time are you driving to Baker tomorrow?" I asked.

"I can't, tomorrow I have to work."

"Biyell, after work I suggest that you drive out there and make this right."

"Uncle Glenn, it's not that easy . . ."

"But you dug this hole, and you fell into it. Don't pull GiGi into this hole with you. She will respect you more if confess and apologize."

I watched him withdraw into a shell. He folded his arms across his knees and buried his head. His contemplation was so loud that I could hear his thoughts as he searched his mental database for the perfect lie. However, his trusted algorithm failed, and I wanted it to fail. Biyell needed to be baptized in the urgency of now.

"Biyell, this isn't going away. Everyone makes mistakes, but it's how you accept responsibility for those mistakes that matters. You have to confront this head-on," I prescribed.

"B-But I don't want to hurt her."

"Biyell, I know you don't, so spare her the public humiliation."

"If I can get her to cancel that transfer, then . . ."

There's that contemplation. "Then you can what? Continue to live two lives?"

"No, that's not what I'm saying . . ."

"Biyell, that is exactly what you're saying, but answer this question." On my crutch, I moved from the counter to the edge of where he sat. "Do you love GiGi?"

"Yes, I love her."

"Do you care about her?"

He shot me a facetious look. "Yes."

"If you love her—if you care about GiGi the way you say you do—then tell her the truth."

"Uncle Glenn, in a perfect world, everything you're saying would work, but what you need to understand about GiGi is it's not that simple."

"Then help me understand."

"Help me, too," Jarvis piped up from behind his laptop.

"Sure, I can drive out there right now and tell her the truth, but that won't be the end of it. She's not one of those women you can fuck over then ride off into the sunset. She's vindictive. She thinks things through. She has a temper."

"And for those reasons alone, you should handle her with respect. Don't sit by and allow these innocent women to slam into each other!"

"It's not that fucking easy!" Biyell's voice traveled across the ceiling. "Listen to me! Tamera was just hired three weeks ago, and GiGi is a ranking supervisor at the state level. Within a week, she will hunt down Tamera and fire her, just to get at me. I knew I was in trouble a long time ago—I saw it in her eyes. I was in it for the sex, but she's a small-town girl who plays for keeps. With the truth will come a financial consequence that I can't afford."

I reached into my pocket and tossed him my cell phone.

"Dial your number," I requested.

"Call my phone?"

"Yeah, dial your phone."

Biyell did as I asked and dialed his phone. Seconds later, his phone buzzed in his pocket.

He shrugged his shoulders. "Huh?"

"Did you have to punch in a code to unlock my phone?"

"No, but I see where you're going . . ."

"Where I'm going is Diana can pick this phone up at any

time, and I don't have to explain a motherfucking thing—I can sleep at night. I have peace! I'm free. When the smoke clears, you may find yourself single again for the first time in years, but you will have peace of mind in knowing you did the right thing. You can finally walk with some integrity—upright, with the peace that I enjoy."

Biyell walked the phone back over to me. "Uncle Glenn, I want to be free; I want to have peace, believe me, I do. I'm tired of living like this. Having to lie every day—this shit is exhausting. The pussy isn't even worth it anymore, but I'm stuck on a cable job and can't afford child support for three kids. You know GiGi is pregnant again. That's the other reason she's relocating here—to be a family and raise our kids. I'm fucked!"

CHAPTER 19

Friday, March 24, 2017
Early morning

You make it easy to be the man that I am because you appreciate my presence; you want me near, you crave my touch. It's easy to be the man that I am when I have a woman who loves the imperfect me . . . Perfectly.

I set the poem I wrote for Diana next to her juice and banana waffles. Watching my wife honor her word to West Jeff Hospital every night has added to the level of respect I have for her; she's true. In a week I will have her all to myself—my heaven. From up the hall, I heard *amazing*—my wife returning from another shift. So, I pressed play on the CD player. The song was "So" by Luther Vandross, which serenaded her right to my arms. I kissed her. She kissed me back, then rested her head on my chest. Like two high school seniors at the prom, we danced. Slow. Close. In love.

"How was your shift?"

"Just how I like it: uneventful. How was your Madden Night?"

"Eventful."

"How so?"

"It was like watching a rerun of a horror movie; you try to warn them but they can't hear you. Then they fall down."

"Is this about Roderick?"

"Yes."

"So that explains why his truck is still outside."

The song ended. My wife took her seat at the table I'd prepared in her honor. She took one bite of the banana waffles and rewarded me with a smile.

"The young lady who co-signed for that truck wanted it back," I explained.

"LaDeisha?"

"No, Shameka."

"Who?"

"Her name is Shameka."

"I never heard of a Shameka."

"I know, because I never mentioned her."

"Why not? We talk about LaDeisha."

"Because I know how you feel about men who cheat."

Diana gave her fork a break and leaned back with her arms folded. "And how do you feel about *men who cheat?*"

"You know how I feel."

"Remind me."

"Well, I feel it's wrong to deceive someone into thinking they're in an exclusive relationship. I don't condone it."

"But how long did you condone it?"

"What do you mean?"

"Roderick has driven that truck for at least two years, which means those women overlapped."

"I knew the entire time."

"And went along to get along?"

"That's not fair, and you know it."

Diana let out a hard fake-laugh. "Was it fair to Shameka and LaDeisha? Huh?" She banged her fist on the table. Some of her juice spilled, but not a lot. "Glenn, help me understand. You laugh and joke, play the video game all night, and just avoid addressing this more serious matter of how could he treat her that way?"

"Well, I do share my opinion about how they're living and have—"

"*They're* living?" She leaned further back in her chair and looked at me as if I were standing too close. "*They're* living? Who else is cheating?"

"Diana, where's your key? I need to hop out to the car right quick; I'll be right back."

"Hop, my ass. Glenn, answer me."

You can't blame me for trying to make a run for it; she had me cornered. Like a tire with a slow leak, I heard the romance leave the room. Yes, I am guilty of one thing and one thing only—I listen, and that's all. I have not cheated on my wife, and if anything, I feel Diana jumped the fence too fast because I have tried my best to talk some sense into these guys. I don't like all of the sneaking around and lies told right in front of me, but these are grown men we're discussing.

"Speak up. What did you say?"

"I said all of them."

Diana stood from her chair and backed me into the refrigerator. Her face swelled with disappointment—not at the guys, but at me. I knew her next question before she cued it up.

"Are you?"

"Diana, stop it . . ."

"Are you?"

"How could you ask me something like that?"

"How could you tolerate men like that? How could you? These men are not casual associates; you guys are very close. Is this what you brag about on Madden Night?" She did the little quote thing with her fingers.

"Diana, I've tried to talk sense into them, and I've used our marriage as an example, but you just said it—these are grown men."

"LaDeisha was here for my birthday party, and now that other woman's truck is outside. Who else has been here when I wasn't home? Better yet, in my house?"

Dammit. I'm stuck at another crucial fork in the road dividing truth from lies. If I tell the truth right here, then I will further incriminate myself. If I lie, then I'm no different than the men in question. Here's what I don't understand—how did this argument become about me? Why am I taking all the heat but not getting any of the pussy that's caught in the middle? All I know is, Diana better back *the-fuck-up-off* me because I have never stepped out on her. Even with one foot, if I wanted to sling dick, I could—but I'm faithful. And this is the gratitude I get?

"None of them have been in the house? How about outside? How many of them have knocked on my door?"

"Well, there was Shameka last month, and Tamera."

"Biyell's wife Tamera?"

"Yes."

"So, in other words, your so-called Madden Night is nothing more than Glenn and the Pimp Bitch All-Stars. And you never mentioned any of this until now."

"Diana, I'm not going to allow you to dump this on me like this. All I can do is share my opinion, and if—"

"Glenn, do I look stupid? What if one of these so-called *men*," she did the quote thing again, "was molesting children? What if? Would you still act as if it's none of your business? Would you still call a child molester your friend because he loves to play a video game?"

"Now wait one got-damn minute! You're taking this shit overboard."

"Would you?"

"Hell no I wouldn't, and you know I wouldn't! And that's not the same thing."

"It is the same because if you didn't agree with the *lifestyle*, they wouldn't get invited to play your game." I wish she would stop with the finger thing. "These guys are your friends because you like them and take no issue with them having multiple mistresses."

"Diana . . ."

"Glenn, you're full of shit. You don't have a problem with their lifestyle, and that is problematic for me."

"Look, you make a very valid point, and no, we wouldn't have a child molester in our group. I get your point, but can you give me some credit for trying to inspire these guys to change? Rasta is free of his double life, and now I'm helping the other guys get free."

"Glenn, did LaDeisha know about this Shameka girl?"

"No, she didn't."

"Are LaDeisha and Roderick still together?"

"No."

"Why not?"

"From what I understand, she broke it off with him."

"As you and I predicted she would once it was time for her to join the family business. Glenn, you didn't do a got-damn thing but regress, and you know how I feel about it—that's why you tried to keep it hush. So I will ask you again. If all of them have a woman on the side, am I woman number one or woman number two?"

"Diana, come on. Please don't go there. You know how I—"

"Glenn, all I know is what you tell me, and this morning proves you only tell me what you want me to know." Slowly, she made her way to the bedroom, but her eyes remained locked on me like a laser. "If my grandmother were here, she would say you are the company you keep, and right now you're hanging out with a pack of whoring men."

"Diana, how could you say something like that to me? You know I am a good man!"

"Glenn, good wouldn't tolerate evil." She locked the door to our bedroom.

CHAPTER 20

Madden Thursday
March 30, 2017
5:20 p.m.

The vibe with Diana this week was like walking down the aisle of a plane watching eyes watch you from behind their seats; like the cabin pressure at thirty thousand feet, like a deafening hum that pops your eardrums . . . but no one says a word. Suppressed anger hummed like a direct flight from New Orleans to Seattle. We said only what needed to be said, but little more after *good morning*. Since last Friday, the entire rhythm of my house has been offbeat; more or less right foot first. That Saturday, Diana was off, but spent most of the day with her sister.

Our normal Saturdays were spent binge-watching Netflix in bed all day, and our Sundays were reserved for listening to novels together. That was Glenn and Diana; that was our marriage. That was prior to her accusing me of being an accessory to infidelity. And hell no I didn't like the way she grouped me in with them, but instead of going back and forth with her about it, I decided to focus all my energy on formulating a master plan—a one-size-fits-all plan, because our marriage and the guys needed fixing. This morning I presented my plan to Diana, and to my surprise, she welcomed the idea.

The truth of the matter is, I love these guys, and she's right—I could have taken a more firm approach with them, but I didn't want to come off as judgmental. So, I'll take my lick, in the same manner that I asked Biyell to take his lick: like a man. As far as the guys are concerned, tonight is still Madden Night and they will still arrive as usual . . . but it will be a very unusual night for them, I guarantee it.

Madden Night
6:00 p.m.

At six o'clock on the nose, all five arrived, but one of them was notably different. Rasta had cut his dreads, and his hands were empty. His head was bald like the palms of your hands, and three shades lighter than his face. I've never heard of a guy cutting his dreads just for the sake of a change-up, so off top I knew something was bothering Rasta in a major way. The other crisis was his empty hands.

"No blunts?" Telly asked as he took his seat at the edge of the couch. "You're sick?"

"I can't believe you cut your hair," Jarvis said.

"Fuck his hair—I can't believe he's here without the weed," Telly sounded it off.

"My last payment to you was last week; I'm taking a break from smoking for a while."

"Damn dude," Telly flushed with aggravation. "We would've appreciated an email; a text, a fuckin' postcard saying no weed tonight. I could've brought some from my stash."

"How does any of this work without weed?" Biyell complained. "We have never been weed-less."

Timothy was first to reach for the PlayStation controller. "This feels weird; like an omen. No weed, plus Rasta has cut his dreads—am I in the right apartment?"

Timothy was right. We have seen Rasta without dreads, but we have never seen Rasta without weed. Maybe it was an omen? Maybe the Earth was drifting away from the sun? Like my marriage, the night got started on the opposite foot.

"Timothy, if you could just hold up one second on starting your match, I would like to call a huddle right quick," I requested.

"Oh shit, let me power up my laptop," Jarvis said.

"No need to, just sit and chill for a second. This will not take that long."

Prior to their arrival, I had placed my cell phone in the middle of the coffee table and moved my favorite stool from the kitchen to the living room, where they wouldn't have any difficulty hearing me.

"Guys, last week was a crazy week, to say the least. I mean, we have never had a week when the spirit of drama paid us all a visit," I began.

"What drama you had?" Timothy asked?

"You have a lil' cutie tucked away?" Telly leaned in.

"You're hiding one?" Jarvis joked.

"No, I not hiding one, but I did catch a lot of heat from Diana. She hates infidelity. I mean, she really hates it—because I gave her reason to."

Shockwaves bounced off the walls like ricocheting bullets.

"You, Uncle Glenn? I can't even see that shit," Rasta said.

Telly looked at Rasta. "Of all nights to go cold turkey on weed, you would pick tonight!"

"Rasta, why don't check inside your shoe, there might be enough weed crumbs in there to smoke," Tim was desperate.

"I'm going dig his dread out the garbage and smoke that!" Biyell stood. "Glenn is about to destroy my hope for humanity, and we don't have shit to smoke?"

"Biyell, have a seat," I ordered him with a finger. "Yes, I had the same level of self-inflicted drama in my life, but far worse. It was a while back."

"How far back?" Rasta wanted to know.

"Thirty-two years, to be exact."

"Cool, I didn't know you then, okay. Proceed." Timothy said.

I'm trying to proceed, but I still can't get used to seeing Rasta with that bald head. It's shiny, too—like Armor All tire shine. And it does feel strange not having any weed to smoke . . . but let me get back to my story.

"I was dating this young lady prior to Diana, and we were constantly on again off again; the typical young love. During one of those times we were off, I met Diana on Canal Street walking with a group of about five other nurses, and so I hollered at her. She gave me her number, we started spending time together, *bing-boom-pow*—we became a couple. The only problem was, Diana wanted to wait until she was married to have sex, and I wasn't trying to hear that—but I knew she was a virgin."

Biyell interjected, "That virgin shit is rare, you have to place them in a whisky barrel and wait it out. I had a bitch one time tell me she—"

"Biyell, chill!" Jarvis yelled. "We've heard that story about the thirty-two-year-old virgin at least thirty-two times! Please continue, Uncle Glenn."

"Like Biyell, I figured I'd wait it out on Diana by fucking this super-fine chick named Derinda. She was the sexiest girl on the Westbank at the time, but she was mean as a pitbull, and love to fight like one. Her momma should've named her Quit-Tina because she would quit my ass on the first Sunday of every month. Then, the moment she heard a rumor of me and Diana out on a date, she would come back. I grew tired of the on-again-off-again—not to mention Diana let me put the finger in—so when Derinda dropped my ass that last time—"

"You proposed to Lady Diana," Rasta concluded.

"Fucking right! It was a short engagement, too. We were married forty-five days later."

"But you were still fucking Derinda?" Telly asked.

"Not at all."

"So you flew straight?" Timothy asked.

"Yes, straight as an arrow."

"Then what was the problem?" Jarvis asked.

"Biyell, do you want to answer that for me?"

"Derinda was pregnant as fuck!"

"Pregnant like Katherine Jackson."

"You didn't tell Diana?"

"Biyell, you know that's too much like common sense."

"No, Unc, you tried to hide the baby?!" Telly was astonished.

"But you're always telling us, *There are a lot of things you can successfully hide, but you can't hide a baby*," Jarvis reminded me.

"And I speak from firsthand experience. Then came baby time. I promised Derinda I would be there for the birth of my first child."

"Were you?" Telly asked.

"Yes, I was there. I figured, what could go wrong? Diana worked in labor and delivery at Tulane, and Derinda was at West Jeff. What could go wrong?"

"Everything," Rasta said.

"What I didn't know at the time is there's this type of nursing called agency nursing where the nurses don't work for the hospital—they report to an agency, and the agency dispatches them where there's a shortage. West Jeff was short on labor and delivery nurses—"

"You better not say it . . ." Biyell shook his head.

"When they admitted Derinda, I was there. When they assigned her room, I was there. When it was time for my daughter to come, I was there. When Diana entered the room to prep for delivery, I was there. If we'd had cell phones, then I would have known that Diana wasn't at the place where I dropped her off for work."

"Let me guess—Derinda didn't know you were married?" Jarvis asked.

"No, and my wife, who I rolled out of the bed with that morning, rolled right into the biggest lie I've never told. I didn't say anything to anyone, and no one asked. Derinda's OB-GYN was running late, and my daughter was in no mood to wait for him."

"Uncle Glenn, please stop this story." Telly slid down to the floor and wallowed in pain.

"Rasta, please check under your armpits; there could be some weed particles, something we could smoke. Anything," Telly pleaded. "I can't listen to this fucked-up story without weed."

"Auntie Diana had to deliver your baby from another woman?" Rasta asked in a weak voice.

"Not only did she deliver my daughter, she maintained her professionalism during the entire delivery. Afterbirth, womb care, even stitching up Derinda. My wife handled that entire delivery. If that weren't bad enough, before she rolled my daughter to the nursery, she wrote out her little name card and taped it to that little glass bassinet. Once they finished all the exams and cleaned my baby, it was Diana who rolled her back to us, snugged in a blanket.

"*She's all cleaned up now. Daddy Braxton, would you like to hold her for the first time?* Diana asked me. She placed my daughter in my arms.

"Just outside Derinda's room, her doctor flipped through some charts before entering the room. Diana turned to Derinda and said, *All right, New Mommy,* that concludes my shift. *I was only called in for this delivery.*

"*Thank you so much for everything you did to make this a safe delivery. I was so worried when my OB-GYN was late,* Derinda told her.

"*You don't have to thank me; I'm just doing my job,* Diana replied. It was then that Diana walked around to the other side of the bed where I stood and kissed me. *Don't worry about picking me up after work, I'll catch a cab. See you when I get home, and congratulations."*

The room was the type of quiet you'd expect from a group of people who just watched someone jump off a bridge. All of them stared off into space. They all had a Derinda or a Diana of their own.

"It took a minute for Derinda to process it; by that time Diana was gone. Shortly after that, I was escorted out of the hospital by the guards. I never saw Derinda or my daughter again, and her family refused to provide me with her location. To this day, I have not laid eyes on my daughter." I felt two tears race down the sides of my face.

"Uncle Glenn, you never shared any of this—in all of this time we spent together," Rasta said.

I swallowed hard. "Over these past few years, I've become very close to all of you. These weekly get-togethers helped me deal with my depression from losing my leg and my child. Last week, Diana tore me a new asshole because I have watched you guys do to other women what I did to her, and I didn't do enough to stop you. But not anymore. Tonight, you will have to make a choice between doing the right thing or continuing down this road of terror."

"I'm not following you, Uncle Glenn," Biyell said.

"Biyell, you have GiGi and Tamera. Telly, you have Yolanda and Erica. Jarvis, you have Monica and her niece, Bri-Bri. Timothy, you had Kayla and Tootsie. Rasta, you had LaDeisha and Shameka. You guys know how close I am to my wife, but we have hardly spoken in a week. The last full sentence she said to me was, *Good would not tolerate evil.* And she was right. The lives you've lived thus far have been cruel, and I can no longer be affiliated with you in your current states."

"Wait, you're kicking us out?" Telly asked.

"Damn, Uncle, you're tapping out on us like that?" Biyell asked with sad eyes.

"Uncle, how you can say you love us in one breath, then just toss us like the garbage in the other?" Jarvis asked.

"All because I didn't bring the weed?" Rasta was confused.

"No, it's all because you refuse to pick one woman and be with only one."

CHAPTER 21

Madden Night
6:30 p.m.

It was harsh coming from me, but I had to say it—if for no other reason than to distance the man that I am from the men in the room. It needed to be said, and the fact that it came from me only added to their shock and awe. I'm not a whore, and fuck the guilt by association bullshit. I refuse to take a charge for pussy I'm not getting. A line has been drawn.

My eyes panned across the room. Their rhetorical questions were spaced two minutes apart, and the space allowed each one to hang in the middle of the room like a wall-mounted fern.

"I get where you're coming from, but I don't think I'm in the same category," Timothy said.

"How the fuck are you not?" Telly asked indignantly. "You're just as fucked up—you forgot I typed up your divorce? The so-called irreconcilable difference was her body fat."

Their behavior was identified and called out. No one wanted to be in that category, but the category was real and relevant. Having two women or more women was a concealed status that they enjoyed, and in many ways I couldn't blame them. Having two sexy women committed to their needs and desires gave them an air of accomplishment and a boost to their self-esteem. I'm not saying it's right; I'm simply explaining why some of us struggle with commitment. There's a little bit more to it than sex, but the sex is major. So too is the stroking of ego, and the word *yes*.

That three-letter word releases endorphins throughout our brains, and the more a woman says *yes*, the more possessive we become. It's in the Bible—it is, right there in the first chapter, in plain view. *God created man in his own image*, and like God, we love worship. A woman who sings praises to only one lord; that's a good woman, but a good god has more than one worshipper. We're sort of like that—some of us. I'm not saying it's right; I'm simply explaining one of the addictive qualities of having more than one devout believer reciting that dopaminergic word *yes* over and over through soft, glossy lips.

Can you move in?

Yes!

Can you suck it out?

Yes!

Can I have some pussy?

Yes!

Can I have a baby boy?

Yes!

Can I watch you dance?

Yes!

Can I hit it from the back?

Yes!

Can I have some pork and beans?

Yes!

Can you wear that yellow sundress today?

Yes!

Can you contact this client for me and reschedule?

Yes!

Can I watch her eat your pussy while I sip a glass of wine?
Yes, baby, yes!

If you have ever wondered how we end up in that category, you can blame it on that three-letter word. Living in New Orleans, it didn't take me long to figure out that the way to my heart wasn't through my stomach. All over this city are women who can cook, but what won my heart was that three-letter word whispered in my ear. Derinda lost out when she started saying the word *no* many times in quick succession. All the men in this room ended up in multiple situations with multiple women because one woman whispered *yes* in his left ear while another repeated the same seductive word in the right.

To call out another man for infidelity is as rare as a fifty-dollar book of food stamps in a Walmart—I haven't seen it in over twenty-five years—but I just called them out, and there's no turning back. The trail of chaos ends in this living room.

It took a total of ten consecutive years before Diana felt comfortable with me, and even then, I never restored her trust back to where it was before my daughter was born. That's how I can say for certain that relationships are like mirrors. Adultery is how you crack that mirror; though the mirror may still be functional, you can always see the cracks. The cracks will never go away. All it takes is the right song, the wrong movie, or a woman with a similar name, and all those nerve endings are reignited.

On the side of my chair was a bag. I placed the bag next to my cell phone, then asked for their attention once more.

"What I'm about to do for you is what I wish someone would have done for me—gotten involved before I caused so much pain. In this bag are five cell phones. I want each one of you to have one. Accept this as a gift. But what's most important is this: only one phone number is saved, and that's my number. You can add other numbers later, but for now, there is only one number."

After selecting a phone, they all returned to their seats, scrolled through their contacts, and there was my name.

"I want each once of you to text me the name of the woman you want to live the rest of your life with - the one that makes you the happiest. Text me her name."

The first person to text was Timothy.

Tootsie

Soon after, other text messages followed.

Rasta: *LaDeisha*

Jarvis: *Monica*

Biyell: *Tamera*

I waited for Telly, but no text came through. "Telly, I'm waiting for you, brother."

"I don't know; it's too hard to choose."

"But you have too."

"I guess I am out before this little game starts—I am not in a position to make that decision."

"Telly, have I ever guided you down the wrong path?"

"No, but this is not a decision I can make. Not right now."

"But you have to make it now."

"Because I can never kick it with you again if you don't? Glenn, this is fucked up - how are you trying to bully us like this -"

"Telly, I am not trying to bully you, I am trying to save you."

"Save me? Save me from what?"

"From becoming what I was."

Telly placed the phone back on the table. "Guys, it was nice knowing all of you, catch y'all online. I'm out."

With that, Telly turned and headed for the door. It was Rasta who went after him, which was only fitting because it was Rasta who invited Telly into the group. I was asking these guys to do something no one ever asked me to do—have some patience, have some respect, have some decency.

For it is in patience that we work through our difference

and grow together. When you have respect for your spouse, then you respect the commitment you have together, and because of that respect, you're less likely to entertain another woman. I asked them to have some decency in how they carried themselves as men, knowing there are some situations you should avoid because of the potential harm it could cause.

After about ten minutes, Rasta returned with Telly. Telly picked up the cell phone and sent me a text:

Yolanda

"Thank you, Telly. Sending me the name was just the beginning. Now it's my turn to send you a text; it's a video. I need each one of you to go to your cars and view the video."

"Then you're going to set off bombs to blow us up, huh?" Jarvis asked.

"Just go watch the video."

CHAPTER 22

7:10 p.m.

THE VIDEO

I know you're thinking I will press a button and blow your head off, but I'm not, because I care about you. I have a little confession to make: it's good news. This is a screenshot of my checking account; the first half of my settlement came in last month for 9.8 million dollars, and I want to invest in you. Each one of you has dreams, but you face unique financial issues. I want to help you, but you have to help yourself. I sold this idea to my wife, and she has agreed to the following.

I asked you to text me the name of the woman you would like to live the rest of your life with in a committed relationship, and now I'm putting forth this challenge. This check I'm holding is for two million dollars. Prove to me that you can commit to one woman for one year, and I will provide the startup capital for your dreams. At the completion of that one year, if you have remained faithful, you will get your share of this check. The check will be divided between all of you who are successful. If you are the only one who has succeeded, then the entire check is yours.

The Conditions:

You must remain faithful to one woman for one full year. There is no loophole—faithful means she's the only one.

If the woman you've submitted by text is your girlfriend, then you must be engaged within this year.

You will be ruled ineligible if the woman leaves you for any reason during the course of this year.

You must end the relationship with your mistress within seventy-two hours and have no further contact with former girlfriends—not even cordial.

If you're found in the act of adultery, you're not only banned from the challenge, you're also banned from our brotherhood.

You cannot tell the woman whose name you have submitted the details of this challenge.

I have almost ten million dollars—that's a lot of money to watch everything you do for one year, so don't think you can cheat me. If you cannot end the relationship with your mistress in seventy-two hours, then drive away right now and keep the phone as a parting gift. If you can, then I ask that you come inside, bring me your old phone, and the challenge begins tonight. The reason I want your old phone is that it's symbolic of an old life, and today you begin a new life that's transparent with the woman you plan to honor.

As a man, I am confronting you as men in a way that I believe will make you stronger and more trustworthy should you accept. This is not a game, and this is not Monopoly money—this is real. I love each one of you, but I will not have my wife looking at me sideways because I hang out with a bunch of whoremongers. I wouldn't make this offer if I didn't believe in you. I only hope you believe in yourself. I'll see you inside. If you decline, then I'll see you in passing.

The choice is yours.

(End of video).

The first person to enter the house and place his phone on the coffee table was Timothy. He'd made his decision to pursue Tootsie and was sure of it. The next person to enter the room was Rasta. He placed his old phone on the table and took a seat. Next through the door was Jarvis, who also placed his old phone on the table. After Jarvis entered the one man I didn't expect to see—Biyell. He'd decided to end it with GiGi. His anguish was severe.

Then I waited.

Then we waited.

After ten minutes, Rasta bolted to the front door, but Telly was gone. Rasta was saddened. I shared his sadness. I also know what it feels like to be trapped between two women—not because they trapped me, but because I trapped myself. As much as it hurts to lose such a good friend, I also know that it's difficult to break a woman's heart. Part of the reason we lie is because we don't want to see her cry.

Once all the guys who had accepted my challenge transferred their important contacts to the new phones, I handed each one of them an envelope. Inside each envelope was a check for twenty-five thousand dollars, to assist them in getting some basic things settled. For instance, Rasta needed a truck to haul his cabinets and wood products to the market. For Timothy, the check could help him tremendously with his housing needs. Though each one of the guys appreciated the envelopes, I could tell their hearts immediately fell on Telly.

Out of all of them, it was Telly who was perhaps in the most financial distress, but it was also Telly who struggled the most with living a committed life. I'm going to miss him because he was a part of us. I'm going to miss his trash-talking, the free legal advice, and that humor. Having said that, I'm so proud of these guys for taking the first step and at least attempting to be with one woman.

Will my experiment work?

I don't know, but it's worth the effort.

If I save one woman from getting her heart demolished the way I nearly ripped out Diana's heart, then this was and will be be money well spent. If only one comes out of this an honest man, then my *Madden* group will continue with myself plus one.

"All right, you guys have seventy-two hours to end that relationship with the other woman, then you're on the clock. I expect to see you back here next Madden Night, and the countdown will begin."

TO BE CONTINUED IN VOL 2 . . .

www.tjnovels.com

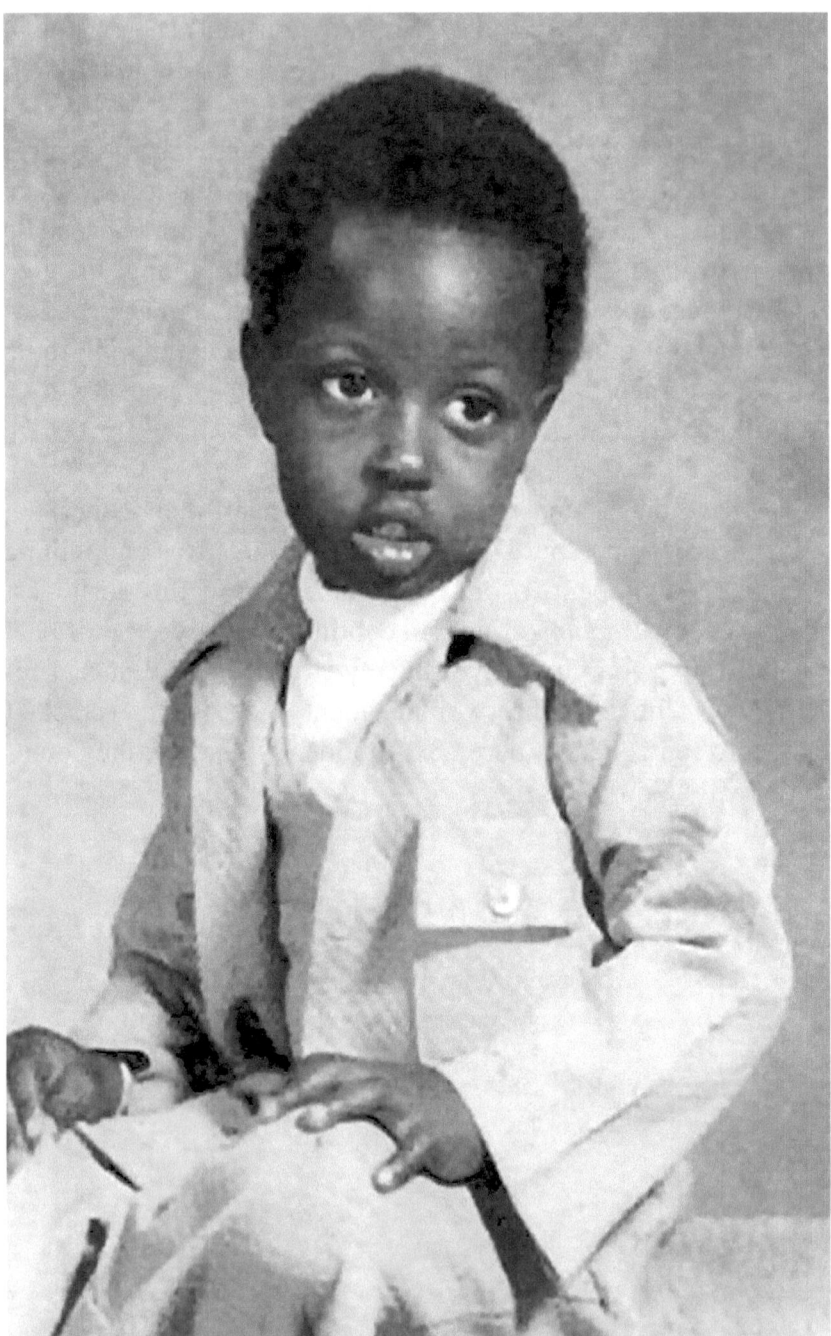

I'm author TJ Spencer Jacques and I have a Doctorate Degree in how to fuck up a good relationship.

Nice to meet you.

Thank you for reading the Infallible Series, your continued support of my novels motivates me every day. This project is a collection of my mistakes as well as the errors of my Madden Brothers: packaged in fiction – but tangible. I make no apologies for the rawness of this content. There are numerous books on the market about men who cheat, but I wanted to explain why we cheat from our point of view, and all the many ways we mentally justify our actions.

I would have you to know that I am the father of five young daughters, and with them in mind I wrote this series as a warning. I am also the father of three sons, as a preventative resource, I wrote Infallible to teach them the consequences of unfaithfulness. I also wrote Infallible for you.

Hope you enjoyed.

TJ SPENCER JACQUES
www.tjnovels.com